La Petite Voleuse

La Petite Voleuse

by CLAUDE MILLER

from an original screenplay by
FRANÇOIS TRUFFAUT
and CLAUDE DE GIVRAY

Translated by JAYNE PILLING

faber and faber
LONDON · BOSTON

First published in France in 1989 by
Christian Bourgois Éditeur, Paris
This edition first published in Great Britain in 1989
by Faber and Faber Limited
3 Queen Square London WCIN 3AU

Photoset by Parker Typesetting Service Leicester
Printed in Great Britain by
Richard Clay Ltd Bungay Suffolk

British Library Cataloguing Data is available

ISBN 0-571-14175-7

CONTENTS

What initially arrests one's attention when glancing over a check-list of François Truffaut's protagonists is the fact that they were, almost without exception, *surnamed*. There was Antoine Doinel, of course, but also Julie Kohler, Bertrand Morane, Julien Davenne, Marion Steiner, Julien Vercel and so forth, not to mention Ferrand, the film director whom Truffaut himself played (without a Christian name) in *La Nuit américaine*. On occasion, too, these slightly implausible surnames (in the cinema, paradoxically, it's easier to believe in and identify with a 'Julien' than with, say, a 'Julien Vercel', perhaps because the character's name tends to remain subordinate in the spectator's mind to that of the actor playing him) were invested by Truffaut with autobiographical connotations. Antoine Doinel's best friend in *Les Quatre cents coups*, for instance, was called René Bigey, as an oblique and probably backhanded compliment to the maternal grandmother, Madame Bigey, of Truffaut's childhood companion-in-arms, Robert Lachenay; and, in an even more ambivalent homage, Lachenay's own surname was given to the adulterous hero of *La Peau douce*, a film which, if one of Truffaut's letters is to be credited, was a reflection of marital difficulties he himself had experienced (and was partly filmed in his own flat).

As the solver of a jigsaw puzzle will start by assembling the squared-off outside edges, so the film-maker must erect a framework that will enable him to develop both his *dramatis personae* and the narrative continuity within which they will evolve: that framework in Truffaut's case was doubtless the naming of his characters. But since, as a rule, the systematic surnaming of fictional characters is very much rarer in the cinema than in literature, and since the New Wave in particular usually spurned such facile short-cuts to social or psychological 'realism', it might be worth attempting to analyse just why Truffaut was so addicted to the device.

The crucial point, surely, is that one's Christian name is one's own, whereas one's surname is first of all that of one's *father* –

crucial, because Truffaut's films were often narratives of Oedipal inspiration, preoccupied with the search for the father, with the outsider's craving for law and authority. As he himself remarked to me, when I interviewed him in 1975, 'If, as I'm sometimes reproached, my films are in contradiction with the age I live in, it's perhaps in the sympathy I continue to have for anyone who must struggle to gain entry to a society from which he was excluded at the outset. It's the theme of *L'Enfant sauvage*, which I made at a time when many young people, scarcely older than the infant in my film, were divesting themselves of their culture, as well as their clothes, and practically going off to live in the forest! If *L'Enfant sauvage* portrayed a creature who was desirous of acquiring an identity – and that he *desired* it, I truly believe – Adèle's concern [in *L'Histoire d'Adèle H.*] was to lose one which she could never consider her own.'

In which light, it can hardly be by chance that when Truffaut filmed the unhappy life of Adèle Hugo, the daughter of the poet and something of an exception in the director's canon by virtue of her pathological need to elude, once and for all, the embrace of a (too famous) father, it was precisely her, and her father's, surname that he chose to excise from the film's title.

As we know, Truffaut's own adolescence was an almost parodically disturbed one: it resembled a classic social worker's case-history, from a broken home (for which he refused to forgive his mother, even on her deathbed) to petty thievery, and from attempted suicide to desertion from the army. He was a feckless, reckless youth who ran away from home *to join the cinema* as others might run away to join the circus. It was only by the intercession of the critic André Bazin that he was rescued from delinquency and possibly outright criminality. Yet, very much later, now a successful film-maker, he was able to describe himself without irony as 'a man of the Right Bank' (if not necessarily of the ideological right wing); and though, like many of his colleagues, he was directly involved in the upheaval of May 1968, his later films were if anything even less overtly political than those which had preceded the *évènements*. Like Antoine Doinel (who, if he was never to be reconciled on-screen with his father, did in the subsequent films of the cycle acquire a father-in-law and a second family through marriage), like Victor of

Aveyron, the tamed *enfant sauvage*, like the unloved schoolchild of *L'Argent de poche* and like, too, Janine Castang, the heroine of *La Petite Voleuse* ('Janine' was the name both of Truffaut's mother and Bazin's wife), what he appeared to be seeking all his life was re-entry, if now on his own terms, into that same society that had once rejected him. Or, to put it more whimsically, what he was seeking was the chance to buy out his father's share in the name 'Truffaut'.

Even in his work (and for this he soon found himself vilified by a few fair-weather fans) there could be detected a progressive gravitation to the centre, the mainstream; a return not so much to the so-called *cinéma de papa*, that complacently retrograde lending-library of literary adaptations that, as a young critic, he had excoriated in a celebrated essay, '*Une certaine tendance du cinéma français*', as to the kind of cinema practised by his true 'fathers', Renoir above all. And in *Le Dernier Métro*, for instance, he would produce that paradoxical object, a good, solidly carpentered 'pre-war' film about the war.

It was, then, as much because he kept the middle ground alive and inhabited as because of his own personal warmth and generosity that Truffaut was not only esteemed but *loved*, loved to a degree that has not been true of any other film-maker before or since. He became, so to speak, the *cinéaste* laureate of his native country, the darling of its actors and (more specifically) its actresses, and arguably the most widely admired director in the world, at least during his own lifetime. That the stories he filmed had a beginning, a middle and an end, generally in that order, that his trademark was a surreptitious rather than an aggressive form of subversion, one born out of sympathy rather than intolerance, meant that he was more than once accused of having sold out to the system. Yet, if we can respect Godard for the ideological distance he covered from his bourgeois upbringing to his deliberate marginalization and eventual self-exile from the blandishments of an industry that he despised as capitalist, corporate and corrupt, so something of the same respect really must be accorded (for his unimpeachable *sincerity*, if nothing else) to Truffaut, whose trajectory, like that of his protagonists, was the exact reverse but no less painful and heroic for that.

Were it not for Truffaut having recolonized the middle ground

with such persuasive, unswaggering conviction, and were it not
for the personal affection that he inspired, it's safe to say that *La
Petite Voleuse* would never have been made. Many directors leave
behind them a drawerful of unfilmed projects; few if any of these
have been realized posthumously with such a fidelity to both the
letter and the spirit of the original.

Just a few weeks before his death in 1984, Truffaut entrusted
two scripts, *La Petite Voleuse* and *L'Agence magique* (the account
of a down-at-heel variety tour in Senegal) to the producer-director
Claude Berri in the hope that either he or another film-maker
might be interested in developing them. Berri, best-known
outside France for *Jean de Florette* and *Manon des Sources*, showed
the former of the two scripts – in fact, a thirty-page treatment
only intermittently *dialogué* – to Claude Miller, who at once
agreed to take the project on. However, as Miller has pointed out
in interviews, it would be misleading to see *La Petite Voleuse* as
merely the film that Truffaut planned to make after *Vivement
dimanche!* Since the original scenario of his very first feature, *Les
Quatre cents coups*, interlinked the destiny of Antoine Doinel
with that of a feminine counterpart, it's clear that the director had
been living, as it were, with Janine Castang throughout his entire
career.

This is confirmed by one of the numerous letters he addressed
to his American *confidante* Helen Scott, dated November 1964, in
which he refers to *La Petite Voleuse* as a forthcoming project,
defining its theme as 'like Ingmar Bergman's *Monika*, the
flowering into femininity and flirtatiousness of a young
delinquent girl, a female *400 Blows*'. Then, the next year, to the
same correspondent: 'I'm in a bit of a state today, I saw my very
first mistress again, the first girl I ever lived with, in 1948, M . . .
She's no longer much to look at, just like me, and she's been in
prison, 3 children, streetwalking and a bit of everything. She lives
in Marseille. I'll go and see her in October to tape an interview
with her on which I will base the scenario of *La Petite Voleuse*.'

Truffaut's motto might have been *women and children first*. He
cared for adult male heroes only if they were, in an unmasochistic
and unmorbid sense, weaklings (notably, Oskar Werner's fey and
flaxen-haired Jules in *Jules et Jim* and the same actor's gentle
fireman in *Fahrenheit 451*). He was especially moved by children

and adolescents because, as he said, everything they do they are doing for the first time (the emblematic image of which might be the amazement of the 'wild child' at his very first sneeze). He realized, too, as few other film-makers have done, that the more of a 'performance' a child gives on the screen, the more closely he approaches the status of the professional actor and the less capable he is of convincing the spectator that he *is* a child. So, whoever would end up filming it, Truffaut or Miller, the success of *La Petite Voleuse* was ultimately contingent on its director's gift for coaxing the tender lucidities and insecurities of adolescence out of his actress's being rather than searing them into her 'performance', for getting her to do everything as though for the first time, no matter how many takes it took.

Miller had already been employed by Truffaut (as an actor in *L'Enfant sauvage*, then as the production manager on all of his films from *Baisers volés* to *Adèle H.*) and has patently been influenced by him as a director. With *La Petite Voleuse* he had the ungrateful task of reanimating the other man's imaginative world. And, whatever else it might be, his version of the script offers a skilful pastiche of Truffaut's mythology and iconography: in the naming of the characters (the middle-aged surveyor to whom Janine offers herself is called Michel Davenne and therefore has the same surname as the protagonist of *La Chambre verte* played by Truffaut himself: its conjunction in a sexual context with the name of Truffaut's mother is surely of some interest to the unreconstructed Freudian in each of us); the emphasis placed on films and books; the police station and reformatory settings (inevitably recalling *Les Quatre cents coups*); the apparition of the open sea (whose untrammelled restlessness was frozen by Truffaut in the final shot of the same film); and, of course, the recurring themes of alienation and revolt – a revolt that cannot, yet again, be regarded as truly *anti*-social in origin, since Janine's thefts are the only means she has of regaining access to the society that abandoned her.

These elements belong to Truffaut, unconditionally. They were delegated, one might even say 'bequeathed', to Miller, who handles them with a respect that is never permitted to compromise his own emotional engagement with the material. What is his, however, and his alone, is Charlotte Gainsbourg, the seventeen-year-old actress who plays Janine. She had worked with Miller before, having been cast as the tomboy heroine of *L'Éffrontée*, his (unacknowledged) adaptation of Carson McCullers's *The Member of the Wedding*. She was, in a way, discovered and nurtured by him as Jean-Pierre Léaud had been discovered and nurtured by Truffaut. And if it's practically impossible to watch *La Petite Voleuse* without thinking of the man who originally intended to make it, without wondering how he might have shot this or that scene, without perceiving it as a homage on Miller's part to one of his own 'fathers', the fact that it seems so much more than merely an act of retrospective piety can be attributed above all to Miller's extraordinary success, like that of Truffaut before him, in catching an adolescent on the wing – *his* adolescent, not Truffaut's, her ugly-duckling charm and gaucheries belonging to his imaginative world and not his mentor's.

Everything, then, is as it should be. *La Petite Voleuse was* a script by François Truffaut but *is* a film by Claude Miller.

Gilbert Adair
1989

La Petite Voleuse

La Petite Voleuse was first shown in the UK at the Prince Charles cinema on 23 June 1989, and in the USA at the Lincoln Plaza cinemas, New York City, in August 1989.

The cast included:

JANINE CASTANG	Charlotte Gainsbourg
MICHEL DAVENNE	Didier Bezace
RAOUL	Simon de la Brosse
ANDRÉ ROULEAU	Raoul Billerey
AUNT LÉA	Chantal Banlier
MAURICETTE	Nathalie Cardone
SÉVERINE LONGUET	Clotilde de Bayser
JACQUES LONGUET	Philippe Deplanche
KEBADIAN	Marion Grimault
RAYMOND	Erick Deshors
PASCOUETTE	Rémy Kirch
MOTHER BUSATO	Renée Faure
YOUNG PRIEST	Claude Guyonnet

Director	Claude Miller
Director of Photography	Dominique Chapuis
Artistic Director	Jean-Pierre Kohut-Svelko
Costume Designer	Jacqueline Bouchard
Editor	Albert Jurgenson
Music	Alain Jomy

Stills courtesy of Orly Films and Valerie Blier/Sygma/John Hillelson Agency Limited.

A co-production from Orly Films, Renn Productions, Ciné Cinq, Les Films du Carrosse, Sédif and the Centre National de la Cinématographie, France.

ONE

1950   A small town in the middle of France.

TEACHER: Mesdemoiselles, you may stand!
*(At these words the thirty girls in the class rise from their desks.
Amongst them is* JANINE, *sixteen years old, hands demurely
crossed behind her back. Their eyes are fixed on the*
HEADMISTRESS, *who has just come in and moves towards the
stage after a nod of greeting to the* TEACHER. *Sliding open the
lid of a large wooden box, the* HEADMISTRESS *empties the
contents noisily on to the desk: thirty small padlocks.)*
HEADMISTRESS: Well, young ladies, here you have thirty
padlocks which are going to cost your parents the mere sum
of 50 francs each! With these padlocks, you will be able to
secure your lockers . . . and I hope I shan't hear any more
about money, watches or articles of clothing stolen from the
cloakrooms. (*Silence. Then, weighing her words:*) This year,
we have a 'black sheep' at Marcelin-Berthelot. A name has
been circulating. And it's the name of someone from this
class.
(Immediately, several girls look towards JANINE, *who doesn't
flinch.)*
But unless I find any evidence, I can only warn the thief to
watch out. Because if there are any more incidences of theft,
I shall be obliged to inform the police. Isn't that right,
Madame Lagache?
(The TEACHER *addressed replies with a fatalistic shrug and an
expression of dismay.)*
And, believe me, the police won't have any of my scruples.
They'll know how to flush out the guilty party. (*Pause.*)
Right; now, in complete silence and in turn, you'll each now
reply 'present' as your name is called.
*(A choreographed set of movements. Each pupil leaves her row to
collect a padlock.)*
Abeille, Chantal?
Present.

3

Bigeaix, Odile?
Present.
Cassagne, Suzanne?
Present.
(SUZANNE CASSAGNE, *a big, gawky, blonde girl, stares pointedly at* JANINE *as she passes.*)
JANINE: (*Muttering to her*) D'you want a photo?
TEACHER: Castang, Janine?
JANINE: Present.

TWO

A few hours later, JANINE *is crossing the street, satchel in hand, moving at quite a pace (like everything else she does) and getting hooted at by passing cars. She arrives at the municipal square, makes for the public toilets, signposted* 'Chalets de Nécessité',* *and disappears inside.*

In one of the cubicles, standing on the toilet seat, she swiftly swaps her satchel for a woman's handbag hidden on top of the cistern. She takes out a cheap little powder compact, opens it, and examines her face. Then she smiles and dabs a little rouge on her lips and cheeks. Behind the door – and we can see only her legs through the gap between the door and the floor – she quickly takes off her ankle socks, slips on a pair of nylons and then high heels.

She comes out of the public toilets. She no longer has her schoolgirl's satchel. In her high heels and nylons, she totters along towards the town centre – her favourite part of town. It's lively, animated, where the most interesting shops and cinemas are to be found. Above a shop doorway, a loudspeaker is broadcasting a current hit record, 'Chanteville', *by Jacques Helian and his band:*

> *A poet loved a young girl,*
> *Lovely as the day at dawn.*
> *The poet with a happy heart*
> *Sang his love out loud.*

* Even for the period, a very old-fashioned, rather quaint appellation for public conveniences.

4

Let's celebrate our love in song,
Our promises, kisses and caresses,
Let's celebrate our love in song,
My beloved, my sweet, my tenderness.

At the Kursaal Cinema, they're playing L'Épave, starring Françoise Arnoul. It looks pretty 'steamy'. JANINE stops to look at the display of stills. In one of them, the actresses's low-cut dress reveals her cleavage. JANINE'S hand goes automatically towards her own rather small breasts. Then her attention is caught by a khaki Dodge, an American Forces vehicle which has just been parked opposite the cinema, in front of a small hotel. In the car a GI and a pretty girl are kissing, and JANINE watches them. She can't help herself: lovers both fascinate and bother her. Her fascination bothers her, and those two especially. They look like they're enjoying themselves. The pretty girl puts a cigarette between the GI's lips. They laugh. Finally, they get out of the car and go towards the hotel, totally absorbed in one another. JANINE has got that odd expression on her face, a kind of fixed smile, which usually signals she's about to get up to no good.

She decides to cross over, to take a look at the Dodge. One of the car windows is open. JANINE looks over to the hotel the couple have disappeared into, then at a carton of Lucky Strikes sticking out of the glove compartment. Quickly her hand reaches forward into the glove compartment and emerges holding the cigarettes. Then she makes off. Jacques Helian and his band are belting out:

Let's sing day and night
Our sighs, desires and secret smiles,
In our room or on the street,
Let's sing about everything we feel.

Further on, in a little street, she stops suddenly, trembling with excitement. The carton of cigarettes won't go into her handbag, so she keeps five or six packets and throws the rest into a grating. Then she sets off again, on the run.

A shop, Les Folies de Paris, displaying women's fashions, with lingerie a speciality. Looking at the display, JANINE'S cheeks go pink. Her hand caresses a little pink nightie, evidently loving the feel of satin this soft. She's in a nervous sweat. She checks that the shop

5

owner – a slim, mustachioed type who's talking to some customers – isn't paying her any attention, then everything happens very quickly. JANINE hoists up her dress, holds the hem between her teeth, tucks the coveted lingerie round her middle, lets her dress fall back in place, and makes for the door. The whole thing takes only a few seconds. The shop doorbell tinkles, and JANINE walks casually away.

THREE

A residential suburb, with chestnut trees throwing their long shadows. A bus drops JANINE off in the church square; she's back in her school clothes. She makes her way down a side street.

Some waste ground, where three kids are kicking a deflated football, and a playful little terrier is running around. Near some small ramshackle houses a battered van is parked. On its side can be read:

A. ROULEAU, CHEESE SUPPLIER.

UNCLE ROULEAU, a well-built fifty year old, is unloading boxes, which he stacks up against a lean-to shed before disappearing into the house. AUNT LÉA – forty, small and sturdy, hard-working – returns from the water pump, carrying a heavy basin full of laundry in her outstretched arms. JANINE appears.

LÉA: (Calling out to her sarcastically) Well, I am sorry, Janine, we didn't hold up dinner for you!
JANINE: (Without stopping) I don't mind. I'm not hungry.
LÉA: (Going over to the washing line) You're never hungry! Anyone'd think you never lived through the war years . . . Put your stuff down and come and give me a hand.
JANINE: All right . . .
(She goes into the Rouleaus' house through the ground-floor window. An empty box serves as a step-up. This is how she usually does it, when she needs to come and go without anyone knowing.

In her corner-room , which contains only a bed and a set of shelves, she hurriedly lifts up her dress, takes out the stolen

6

lingerie and stuffs it behind the bed. LÉA *is still shouting from the yard.*)

LÉA: D'you hear me, you lazy great lollop? Now's not the time to start mooching about!

JANINE: OK, OK, I'm coming!

(*She goes into the kitchen-dining room of the tiny dwelling. Sitting at the table,* UNCLE ROULEAU *has pushed aside what's left of his meal. He's concentrating on his favourite hobby: the pantograph (a little gadget which, by an ingenious mechanical device, can reproduce line drawings from a model). This evening, he's 'drawing' the cathedral at Chartres. His glasses keep sliding down his nose.* JANINE *nicks an apple from the sideboard.*)

JANINE: Evening!

ROULEAU: (*Without raising his eyes from his drawing*) Who're you saying good evening to? The dog?

JANINE: (*Pouting; it costs her dear to be polite*) Good evening, Uncle.

ROULEAU: Have you had your dinner?

JANINE: Yes, I had a snack.

ROULEAU: A snack isn't dinner. Not that I care . . . if you want to keep your bean-pole figure.

JANINE: What's a bean-pole figure?

ROULEAU: Well, it's the New Look, all skin'n'bones. Don't you know about the skin'n'bones look? That's how your mother was, kept fainting all over the place from not eating.

JANINE: But what if it was to make her more attractive?

ROULEAU: Well, I suppose you could say that if it was to make herself attractive, she certainly succeeded! And you're the living proof.

JANINE *shrugs her shoulders, muttering: 'I don't care.' She's used to sarcastic remarks about her mother.* LÉA *comes in from the yard, a bundle of damp laundry in her arms.*)

LÉA: (*To* JANINE) So what are you up to now?

(*She hurls the bundle of laundry forcefully at* JANINE, *who catches it.*)

JANINE: (*Yelling*) 'But I was just coming out to help you!

LÉA: What a performance! Why don't you bring on the violins!

JANINE: But I don't play the violin!

ROULEAU: Stop it, you two. You're going to make me get it wrong! Look at that. It's all crooked now!
(*He's erasing and crossing out.* LÉA *comes to look at the drawing over his shoulder and compares it with the original.*)
LÉA: It's a good likeness, though.
ROULEAU: Of course it's a good likeness, otherwise there's no point. I'm not trying to be Picasso. It's a likeness I'm after.
JANINE *is amused at this. But not for long. For, as she goes to hang out the laundry, she notices a car arriving in the yard. She looks deeply uncomfortable. It's the* PROPRIETOR *from Folies de Paris who gets out of the car, looking very fierce and extremely determined . . .*

A few moments later, JANINE, *ghastly pale, waits for the sky to fall in.* LÉA *is very worked up.*)
LÉA: I'm not getting worked up, Monsieur, I'm simply asking if you've got any proof!
PROPRIETOR: (*Trying to keep calm*) I do, Madame. A client who saw your daughter.
LÉA: (*Cutting him short*) First of all, Janine isn't my daughter, she's my niece! Secondly, this client better come and tell me so herself, if she can look me in the eye!
PROPRIETOR: Look you in the eye!
ROULEAU: (*Still sitting with his pantograph; he tries to be conciliatory*) Listen, Léa, if everyone talks at once, we're not going to get anywhere.
PROPRIETOR: I'm telling you, your niece slipped the nightie under her dress, and that fact just happens to coincide with what my top saleswoman, Éliane, told me about a stole going missing last week and . . .
LÉA: Well, excuse my ignorance, but I don't understand what you mean by 'slipped under her dress' . . . and anyway, I've no idea what a 'stole' is.
PROPRIETOR: Madame, a stole is . . . look, today it's a matter of a little imitation satin nightie worth about 140 francs, but last week it was a fox fur worth over a thousand that she swiped!
LÉA: Over a thousand? What kind of fox is worth 'over a thousand'?

8

(*Janine's corner-room. Her bed in the foreground. The three
enter the room.*)

ROULEAU: Well, you can search the room, then we'll see!
That's her bed! These are her schoolbooks! What do you
want, Monsieur? A look behind the bed? Well then, we'll
look behind the bed! (*He moves the bed. Silence. Astonished
dismay. In a recess, the 'swag': pens, inkwells, pencil boxes,
books, tools, cheap paste jewellery, cartons of American
cigarettes, lots of clothes and underwear, most still with the price
tags attached. Everything* JANINE *has stolen over the last few
months.*) Bloody hell!

PROPRIETOR: (*Picking out articles of clothing on the kitchen
table*) That skirt belongs to me, that's the fox fur . . . (*He
waves them under Léa's nose.*) You wanted to know what a
stole worth over a thousand was like, Madame Rouleau?
Well, here you are. And this here, you want to tell me it's
not from Folies de Paris? Look, the price tags are still on.
(*His voice takes on an insinuating tone as he addresses*
JANINE.) Tell me, young lady, am I right in thinking
you've got a taste for luxury lingerie?
(*Feeling very guilty,* JANINE, *expressionless, kneads her arms
– a nervous gesture she has when there's no escape.* LÉA *and*
ROULEAU *are very shaken up,* ROULEAU *especially; he sits
on a stool, head in his hands. The* PROPRIETOR *gathers the
articles of clothing together.*)
Well, I've had enough fun here . . . all that's left is to
inform the police. I suppose you don't have a telephone?

LÉA: (*Trying to appeal to him*) Do you really think . . .?

PROPRIETOR: (*He looks at them, troubled. He weighs things up,
hesitates, then, in a condescending tone*) Well, I'm no brute
. . . but it's only because we're both in business, you
understand? You're lucky it's me.

LÉA: Oh, thank you, Monsieur, thank you so much. (*To*
JANINE) And how about you? It wouldn't kill you to say
thank you, either, or would it?
(JANINE *remains tight-lipped.*)

PROPRIETOR: Honestly, kids these days! The pair of you are
going to have to take a hard line, believe you me. (*As he
leaves*) In any case, the main thing, as far as I'm

9

concerned, is that I've got my goods back.

JANINE: Yeah, even the stuff that's not his!
(*He doesn't hear her. Whack!* LÉA *clouts her across the face* . . .
On account.

As soon as the shopkeeper has gone,* ROULEAU *launches himself
at* JANINE – *the sudden clumsy violence of a weak man. He
chases her round the little flat.* JANINE *tries to dodge him, trips
and knocks against the table. A basin clatters down. Crash!
Bang! Clunk!*)

LÉA: Stop it, André, you'll kill her, with those dirty great paws
of yours! Stop it!
(ROULEAU *is shaking* JANINE. *He's violently angry, but at the
same time there's something very sad about him.*)

ROULEAU: What's got into you? For God's sake, JANINE,
what's wrong with you? Bloody hell! I don't want any more
aggravation like that from shopkeepers, do you understand
me? (*He sends her flying against the wall, stumbles in a daze
towards the little corner-room, and says to* LÉA:) Just look, look
at all this stuff! It must be worth a small fortune! What are
we going to do with it? (*He shouts.*) What on earth are we
going to do with it?

FOUR

*On the outskirts of town, the Workers' Allotments – a labyrinth of little
vegetable plots in which 'weekend gardeners' are digging and weeding.
In the field which borders the allotments,* LÉA *and* JANINE *are
pushing a bike along. The 'thief's loot' is packed in boxes in the front
pannier;* JANINE *is looking sorry for herself.* LÉA *stops at one of the
allotments.*

LÉA: Hey! Pascouette? Are you there?
(*In one of the allotments, a man straightens up over his
chrysanthemums; he doesn't look very accommodating.*)

PASCOUETTE: Yeah.
(*Dressed in vest and dungarees, in his forties; small, sharp,
fierce-looking, a real 'stud'.* LÉA *and* JANINE *open the gate and
go towards him.* AUNT LÉA *kisses him, her eyes sparkling.*)

LÉA: Hello, love. (*She gestures towards* JANINE.) Just look at that! We just don't know what to do with her any more! Her latest game is stealing stuff from the shops.

PASCOUETTE: So?

LÉA: So, Rouleau's sick to the back teeth. And you can imagine, if it gets round. He said, 'You'll have to go to Pascouette; burn it all.'

PASCOUETTE: He's got a nerve, your husband, and you can tell him so from me. Thinks I've nothing better to do, does he?

LÉA: Those chrysanthemums of yours are coming up beautifully. Look at that; they're as big as cauliflowers.

PASCOUETTE: They're coming along, coming along. So they should! I spend my nights picking caterpillars off them. I'll never be ready for All Saints' Day, with all your mucking about!

(*The three of them proceed along the rows of flowers and vegetables.*

It's a great thing, a bonfire. A real show. There's something almost luxurious about it. All those expensive things going up in flames: stockings, underwear, packets of American cigarettes. Their colourful packets eaten by the flames. At the bottom of the garden, PASCOUETTE *uses a garden fork to poke the fire in the brazier;* JANINE *stands by silently, fascinated. In front of the wooden shed,* LÉA *watches them as she sips a glass of wine.* JANINE *is sullen.*)

JANINE: All you've got to do is let me leave school. Let me get a job.

LÉA: What kind of job? Where?

JANINE: At the dairy. With Uncle Rouleau.

LÉA: (*With a look of heavy disbelief*) At the dairy? Oh yes, I can just see that! What on earth put that into your head? Have you seen the state of your uncle?

JANINE: What d'you marry him for, then?

LÉA: Because I thought that with him running a business, we'd do all right for money. If only I'd known.

(PASCOUETTE *has abandoned his task and come to sit next to* LÉA, *who places her hand affectionately on his. They're quite open in front of* JANINE, *who turns her back on them.*)

Go on, have a good sulk! She does nothing but cause us trouble, and then she sulks! (*To* PASCOUETTE:) She pinches money from us as well, right out of my purse! And d'you know what for? To go to the pictures, to see *Le Bal des sirènes*. All those girls swimming about with feathers stuck up their arse, swimming pools, water fountains, all that rubbish.

JANINE: (*Bristling*) You've no idea what you're talking about. It was an operetta, about rich people. It was beautiful. There were loads of songs as well.

LÉA: Be quiet! It was a disgusting film, I'm telling you. (*A pause.*) And then there's the boys: I shan't go on.

(JANINE, *wide-eyed.*)

Don't come the innocent with me! So it wasn't you I saw Thursday with the boys from the glass-works! What a carry on! My God! How could you go messing about with them like that?

PASCOUETTE: (*Chipping in, deadpan*) Well, her mother was just the same.

LÉA: You're right, that's Louise all over. Music, the pictures, the pictures, music. (*To* JANINE:) And you saw what that got her, didn't you, at Liberation?

JANINE: Yeah, it's easy enough to speak badly of people when they're not there. You wouldn't say that to her face, not to my mother.

PASCOUETTE: Where would you be without your aunt and uncle Rouleau, then? Can you tell me that?

JANINE: (*Muttering darkly*) Anyway, one of these days I'm going to be with her again.

LÉA: Think you can count on it?

JANINE: Of course I can. She wrote to me.

LÉA: What a lie!

JANINE: (*Insistently*) Yes, she did. She wrote to me. She wrote to say where she was in Italy, and that I was going to join her there!

LÉA: A lie, I tell you! Where's the letter, then?

(*Silence.*)

Go and get it. I want to see it!

PASCOUETTE: If your mother had wanted to write to you any

time over the last five years, don't you think she would have already?
(*Nothing hurts like the truth.* JANINE *clings on to her lie like grim death.*)
JANINE: (*Muttering*) Well, she did write to me. It's the truth.
LÉA: Where's the letter, then?

FIVE

The following Sunday. Itinerant market traders in their vans have set up stalls in the church square. At the dairy van, JANINE *is helping the Rouleaus. She's competent and serious in her work. She wields the measuring spoon authoritatively as she scoops out some cream. She can slice a quarter pound of butter from the block, judging purely by eye. She wraps the packages neatly in newspapers current at the time* (Radar, Samedi Soir). UNCLE ROULEAU *weighs a portion of cheese for* M. FAUVEL, *who runs the little restaurant in the square, Les Fauvettes.*

ROULEAU: And the newspaper comes free! (*He notices the headline in the newspaper wrapped around the cheese.*) 'What would you do if the Red Army occupied France?' Good question! Wouldn't bother me! I hope the Russkies'll be along soon, to sort things out. We wouldn't be any worse off!
FAUVEL: I thought you were a Gaullist, Rouleau?
ROULEAU: De Gaulle or Stalin: one or the other! There's nothing to choose between them.
LÉA: That's typical! Weaklings like him always go for the tough 'uns!
(*As she says this, she comes out from behind the stall and moves away.* JANINE *watches her. Carrying a basket full of enormous cheese sandwiches which she's just made, her aunt stops at Pascouette's stall, a few feet away. Break-time.*)
FAUVEL: (*Meantime, to* ROULEAU) Well, my friend, if that's how you think, we've got a fine future in store!
ROULEAU: The best years are over now, Fauvel. At least during the war we were writing the History of France. I feel let down by Liberation, I do.

(*At the same time – he can't help himself – he has to look over at Pascouette's stall. The dairywoman's white overall presses up close against the blue apron of the market gardener. It's obvious, even from a distance. Suddenly, in front of the dairy-van, a customer turns round.*)

CUSTOMER: Look, over there! It's the 'angel-maker'.★

(*She gestures with a glance over to the other side of the square. Two women are coming out of a small house. One is elderly, wearing a shopkeeper's overall, the other is a pale young woman, looking very distressed. JANINE looks over in their direction, while the gossip continues at Rouleau's stall.*)

Poor Mado, it was about time.

ROULEAU: Well, in any case, Mother Busato's not done so badly out of her day's work.

(*The old woman and MADO part company in front of the tobacconist's.*)

OLD WOMAN: (*To MADO*) You'll find the money all right. (*She follows young MADO with her eyes, then goes into her shop.*)

ROULEAU CUSTOMER: I'd give a lot to know how much she makes.

★ '*Faiseuse d'anges*': a colloquial euphemism in a Catholic country for a back-street abortionist.

ROULEAU: How do you think she got the tobacconist shop? (*He brandishes his cutting knife, with a twist of the wrist.*) Like that! Sending little souls to heaven.

(JANINE *doesn't miss a bit of it. She's fascinated with all this, finds it all very interesting. Especially* ROULEAU's *conspiratorial air as he confides to his customers.*)

It seems you have to say to her: 'Good day, Madame Busato. I'd like a box of matches, family size, please.' And then you follow her into the back room. That's the pass-word.

(*A moment later,* JANINE *appears in the tobacconist shop.*)

JANINE: Good day, Madame Busato. I'd like a box of matches, family size, please.

(*Mother Busato's sharp eyes evaluate the age and condition of the girl. It doesn't take long.*)

MOTHER BUSATO: And would you like to feel the back of my hand, too?

(JANINE *is noisily ejected from the shop. By the end of the morning, the market vans have started packing up.* JANINE *prowls around the church. She goes up to an open window and chances a look inside. It's the vestry kitchen. The elderly sacristan puts a pewter bowl on the table – the proceeds from the collection – coins and notes. The* PARISH PRIEST, *still dressed for the mass, puts the money into a biscuit tin. He's a very young priest, with close-cropped hair and a rough peasant's face.* JANINE *spies on him from behind the window. The* YOUNG PRIEST *locks the biscuit tin in the dresser.* JANINE *now moves away from the window and goes over to lean against the wall of the church, eyes still trained on the vestry. She takes a used cinema ticket from her pocket.*

In the vestry kitchen, an hour later. The YOUNG PRIEST, *now dressed in a simple cassock, is peeling potatoes for soup, with the* SACRISTAN *beside him. Suddenly the window is blown open by a gust of wind. The* SACRISTAN *gets up to close it. But somehow the window won't close properly. The* SACRISTAN *leans over, examining the window catch, and realizes that it's blocked by a cinema ticket.*

Night. The tobaccanist sign over Mother Busato's shop is switched off. In the deserted square, JANINE *moves along the*

*church wall, hurrying as she approaches the vestry, which is in
total darkness.* JANINE *slips in easily. The window, 'fixed'
earlier, opens as planned. Quickly: the dresser.* JANINE *opens the
top cupboard door, reaches up to take the biscuit tin. Clap! A hand
brutally grabs her wrist. It's the* SACRISTAN.

A moment later, the YOUNG PRIEST *rushes up, buttoning his
cassock, still half asleep. He beats at the door. The* SACRISTAN
opens it; he's very worked up.)

SACRISTAN: It's the thief, father. But it's a girl!

YOUNG PRIEST: A girl thief?

SACRISTAN: Yes, it's Janine, the dairy couple's niece. I've locked
her in the coal cupboard. (*He opens the door of a cupboard under
the stairs. A ray of light.* JANINE *can be made out, huddled next
to a heap of small coal briquettes.*) Come on out, you!

(JANINE *scrambles out of the cupboard. She keeps her eyes on the
floor The* SACRISTAN *pushes her roughly into the kitchen. He
rushes over to the telephone.*)

Yvonne? Can you get me the police station, please? It's about
a theft. Yes, I'll wait.

(*In the kitchen,* JANINE *and the* YOUNG PRIEST *are alone
together for a moment. He seems bothered by the fact that she's a
girl, and so young at that . . .*)

YOUNG PRIEST: But why did you do it? Can you tell me?

JANINE: I don't know.

SACRISTAN: I hope that you're ashamed?

JANINE: Yes.

YOUNG PRIEST: But what exactly are you ashamed of? Yourself?
Or what others might think of you?

JANINE: (*Hopefully, thinking it's the right thing to say*) Of what
others might think of me?

(*Silence. The* PRIEST *looks at her; she could be his little sister.
Then* JANINE, *looking straight at him, speaks suddenly.*)

Ask me for anything you want. I'll say 'yes', and then you can
let me go.

(*An hour later, the police station, gloomy and smoke-filled. Alone
in her 'cage', sitting on the narrow little bench,* JANINE *looks
about her. A policeman is throwing briquettes into the stove. Three
others are having a meal-break, in silence. The* SERGEANT,

16

*who's half asleep, is writing at a little table covered in ink stains,
taking statements from the* SACRISTAN *and the* PRIEST.
*They're all talking in hushed tones as though there were a dead
body in the room. Standing next to them is* UNCLE ROULEAU.
*He too looks intimidated, as though he were the guilty one. From
time to time he raises his eyes to look at* JANINE. *His expression
makes her feel ashamed. The* YOUNG PRIEST *looks at*
JANINE *too – brief, furtive glances. When a man looks at her
like that,* JANINE's *reflex is to smile back, but, given the
circumstances, it ends up as an odd grimace.
The* YOUNG PRIEST *is still eyeing her, as though he's never
seen anything like her before.* JANINE *is fed up of keeping her
eyes down, so she looks back at him, and this time gives him a
real smile. Suddenly, the group dissolves: the* SERGEANT, *the*
SACRISTAN, *the* PRIEST, ROULEAU. *The* PRIEST *puts his
beret back on and knots his scarf, whispers a few more words to*
ROULEAU, *shakes his hand, then leaves, with a last little look
in Janine's direction. The* SERGEANT *opens the 'cage' and
brings out the young criminal.*)

SERGEANT: You should thank the priest. He doesn't want to
make a formal complaint. He says it would be using a
sledgehammer to crack a nut. So I'm releasing the 'nut'.
(*He pushes her towards* ROULEAU.)

(*On the steps of the police station, the* SERGEANT *admonishes*
ROULEAU.)
You can deal with this in your own way, but I don't want to
see her around here again. Do I make myself clear? Good
night, then, André.

ROULEAU: Good night, Lucien.
(JANINE *and her uncle go off into the night. Dead silence
between them. Then suddenly* ROULEAU *gives her a kick in the
backside. A big kick.*)
Bloody little bugger!

JANINE: Owwww! It's not fair! What's wrong with you?
(*Silence again.*)

ROULEAU: Jesus H. Christ! Just what in hell is that all about?

JANINE: It's not 'about' anything. I just want to go out and earn
a living.

17

A small newspaper ad, circled in thick pencil: 'Longuet, 11, avenue du Parc: housemaid wanted; ref. reqd.' A stylish neighbourhood in a large town. A typically bourgeois street. Exterior of a wealthy-looking building. Imposing entrance. Dressed 'correctly', newspaper folded under her arm, JANINE *checks the address: '11, avenue du Parc'. It's the right place. But as for 'ref. reqd' . . . The young girl assumes an expression of guarded optimism.*

A hesitant push at the door, which opens. JANINE *makes her 'entrance' rather tentatively, rigged out in a white apron over a black skirt and carrying a soup tureen as if it were the holy sacrament. The new maid moves through the splendid, bourgeois dining-room like a spectral presence in front of her new employers, the Longuets, who are seated at the table with a couple of friends.* JACQUES LONGUET, *a good-looking man of thirty-five, is in full flow, talking business.*

LONGUET: So I said to him, 'Look, old man, if we're going to use concrete for all four arches, then Bridges and Highways are simply going to throw the whole project back in our faces, and that'll be that.'
 (*Without looking at anyone,* JANINE *hesitates as she walks round the table, as though wondering where to put the soup tureen.*)
JANINE: (*Announcing in a funereal tone*) I've made some broth.
 (*She continues to circle the table in the heavy silence that follows. As she leaves the room, without turning round, she adds in an audible whisper, a sinister:*) Enjoy the meal, ladies and gentlemen.
 (*Exit. In her confusion, she knocks her shoulder against the glazed door to the hall. The faces of those around the table display a mixture of amusement and astonishment.* JACQUES LONGUET *is about to signal his surprise, but his wife,* SÉVERINE (*twenty-five, pretty, pleasant, witty*), *says with a smile:*)
SÉVERINE: Our new maid!
 (*A few days later. In the living room,* SÉVERINE *puts a record*

*on, Jacques Helian and his band with a version of the swing hit
'Hey di ho'.*

> Singing Hey di ho
> Hey di ho-ho-ho
> The sky seems bluer to me
> Ho ho . . .

Moving in time to the rhythm, SÉVERINE *places a pretty
bouquet of roses in a vase on the dining-room table. At the same
time, in her attic room,* JANINE *thrusts a single rose into a tooth
mug. The room is sparsely furnished – there's no water or
electricity – but clean. And at least it's a room of her own,
compared to the 'corner' she had at the Rouleau house. She
continues fixing up her new home. Then she goes to the window,
leaning out on her elbows, high up on the top floor, under the
eaves. Sounds of busy traffic.* JANINE *is exhilarated. Séverine's
record player is heard from afar.*

> I see life
> In a new light
> When I'm singing Hey di eh
> Hey di ho-ho-ho

Deftly pushing the door open with her behind JANINE *enters the
kitchen. A few days later. The young maid has grown more
confident. Clack! A tea tray is placed on the draining board. Two
cups are quickly washed.*

*Like before, at the 'Chalets de Nécessité': a pair of low-heeled
shoes are swapped for a pair of high heels. The maid's apron and
black skirt are shoved hastily into a low cupboard. The hem of a
pretty dress can be seen. Like a young soldier on leave anxious to
get out as soon as possible,* JANINE *has her 'civvy street' clothes
on beneath her uniform.*

*In the street, Janine's legs amongst those of other passers-by.
They stop as she arrives at a cinema. A vivid poster for a
romantic musical:* Passion Eternelle, *a Schumann biopic, with
Cornel Wilde and Katharine Hepburn.** JANINE *is tempted.*

*No one, specific film is intended here; it's a deliberate jumble of films to suggest a
particular type of Hollywood romantic musical biopic.

We now see all of her: make-up, all dolled-up, a child disguised as a woman.

Waves of romantic music. Sentimental dialogue. In the cinema, JANINE *is sitting in the second or third row, head tilted back, mouth agape. Two youths come and sit near her, one right next to her, the other in the seat behind. They begin their pick-up routine. But she wants to be left alone. She shrugs off their comments, removes the odd wandering hand. They persist. She looks for another seat. A little further along her row, she spots a man of around forty, bespectacled, in suit and tie, sitting next to a respectable looking woman.* JANINE *gets up and moves into the seat next to the couple. The man looks at her quizzically: there are several other empty seats on that row.*

A luminous beam from the projection box. A little later. The respectable-looking woman suddenly looks at her watch in the light from the screen then gets up and leaves. So she's not the man's wife. JANINE *is embarrassed at having sat down next to this man who's by himself. But it doesn't matter; immersed in the film he doesn't pay her any attention.*

A crescendo of music. The picture's over. The lights go up. The audience get up to go. Back to JANINE. *She's fast asleep, leaning on the shoulder of the man next to her.*)

THE MAN: Miss . . .

(*Embarrassment. He'd like to leave. Cautiously he disentangles himself, holding her up so she won't fall sideways. She half wakes up, then goes back to sleep on his shoulder.*

A few seconds later, in the aisle leading to the exit.)

JANINE: Look, I'm really sorry . . .

THE MAN: (*Reassuring her gently*) No, it's quite all right, don't worry.

JANINE: Was I asleep for a long time?

THE MAN: Quite a while.

JANINE: (*Hesitating; she can't stop yawning*) Oh dear, how embarrassing! And I'm still sleepy.

THE MAN: What you need is a good cup of coffee; that'll wake you up. There's a café over the road.

(JANINE *and* THE MAN *are now seated in the back of the café.*

The waiter arrives with a Coke for her and a glass of milk for him. JANINE *starts sucking through her straw.* THE MAN *watches her, amused. She offers him her Coke.*)

JANINE: D'you want some?

THE MAN: Do you think I should?
(*She gives him a look of encouragement, but he doesn't respond. He drinks some all the same.*)
All right, I'll try it.
(*He makes a face.* JANINE *laughs, delighted.*)
Oh, no, it's awful! You'll never get me to drink this stuff.

JANINE: (*She looks at him and then*) Don't you like anything that's new?

THE MAN: (*Surprised*) No, it's not that. What makes you think so?

JANINE: I don't know, maybe because of the film; it's pretty old-fashioned. Well, I mean, it's set in olden times.
(*A silence. He drinks his milk. He looks gentle, unassuming and a bit pathetic.*)
And you go to the pictures by yourself.

THE MAN: (*Gently*) And . . .? So do you.

JANINE: Well yes, I know, but it's normal for me. When I go, it's to meet people.'

21

THE MAN: Oh?

JANINE: Yes. And anyway, it was a film more for women than for men.

THE MAN: Oh no, I don't agree with you there. And the proof is that neither my wife, nor my daughter – who's around your age – would come with me.

JANINE: Don't they like the pictures?

THE MAN: Yes, but not classical music.

JANINE: But you do?

THE MAN: (*Nodding emphatically*) Yes, I do . . . a great deal.

JANINE: Why?

(*That's a difficult question to answer. He reflects for a moment, wanting to be precise.*)

THE MAN: Well . . . because music is rather like poetry or painting. In life, everything finally gets old, dies out or disappears, and that's sad, don't you think?

(*JANINE agrees, flattered by the fact that this man, a stranger, is talking to her about such serious matters.*)

Well, you see, I think that music is a way of trying to hold on to these moments, to store them up in your memory, so you won't forget, all those things which otherwise would just fade away.

JANINE: You mean it's to remind you of people's lives, is that it?

THE MAN: Yes, that's it, exactly. People, but also everything they cared about.

(*He looks at her warmly. She gives him a lovely smile.*)

JANINE: Are you a musician, then?

THE MAN: Oh, no. I work at the Town Hall. In the Land Registry Department. It's not that interesting, but twice a week I conduct a choir. It's no big deal, though. And what do you do? Are you a student?

JANINE: Oh, no. I've got a job.

(*He waits for her to tell him what it is. She's a little thrown by this.*)

I'm at an Institute.

THE MAN: What kind of Institute?

(*The man at the next table has a newspaper sticking out of his pocket; JANINE spots the word 'beauty'.*)

JANINE: It's a really great place, a 'beauty' place.

THE MAN: Oh, you mean a Beauticians' Institute?
JANINE: That's it.
(*He seems pleased for her.*)
THE MAN: So you're training to be a cosmetician?
(*Another word she doesn't know.*)
JANINE: (*Evasively*) Sort of . . . anyway, I'm really glad I met
you. Usually when I'm with a grown-up I'm either being told
what to do or being made a pass at.
(*He covers his embarrassment with an understanding expression.*)
Can I ask you a question?
THE MAN: Of course.
JANINE: If I tell you my name, will you tell me yours?
THE MAN: I'll tell you right now. I'm called Michel . . . Michel
Davenne.
JANINE: And I'm Janine. Janine Castang. Not very pretty, is it?
THE MAN: (*With sincerity*) Why? No, no. Janine's a nice name.
It's sweet, but it's also determined-sounding.
JANINE: (*Radiant*) D'you think so?
(*From where she is she can see the entrance to a small hotel, the
furtive comings and goings of a prostitute.* MICHEL *sees her
looking and misunderstands, worried that she might be shocked.*)
MICHEL: Yes, well, it's not a very nice neighbourhood round
here. It'd be better if I took you home. My car is parked
quite near here. Where do you live?
JANINE: Avenue du Parc. Number 11.
(*A well-to-do neighbourhood. He's impressed.*)
MICHEL: Well, I don't know the building, but avenue du Parc,
you're doing well there.
JANINE: (*With false modesty*) Yes, I know.
(*A few moments later, his '202' draws up in front of the
Longuets' apartment building.*)
MICHEL: Well, here we are.
(*Silence.* JANINE *seems lost in thought for a moment.*)
JANINE: (*In a low voice*) If we see each other another five times,
the fifth time you're going to ask me. So why don't you ask
me right now?
(*Silence.*)
MICHEL: How old are you?
JANINE: I'm old enough. (*A pause.*) My God, it's like being at

the police station. I'm sixteen, and I've never done it, if that's what you want to know!

(*Silence*.)

MICHEL: (*Calmly*) I wouldn't want to be the first lover in a young woman's life.

JANINE: (*Very disappointed*) Oh. Not even with me? (*A pause, then she mutters:*) But somebody's got to be the first.

(*He looks at her, at once disconcerted yet moved.*)

MICHEL: Don't think that I don't find you attractive, Janine. On the contrary, I find you very appealing . . .

JANINE: Well, then? I find you attractive too.

MICHEL: No, no. It's a question of principle.

JANINE: A 'principle', that means 'never'?

MICHEL: Yes, that's it. A principle is sacred.

JANINE: Like the Coke?

MICHEL: What?

JANINE: (*Explaining herself*) You said you'd never drink it.

MICHEL: Oh, yes, sort of like that. Love is a serious matter, really it is. No, I just couldn't go against my principles.

JANINE: (*Miserably*) Well, then, don't. It doesn't matter. Let's forget I ever said anything.

(*Silence*.)

MICHEL: We can see each other again if you want to.

JANINE: (*Her smile returning*) Oh yes, that'd be nice!

MICHEL: Would you like to come to the choir?

JANINE: Oh, I'd love to. When?

MICHEL: Well, tomorrow maybe, at seven, seven thirty. Behind the town hall. Do you know the Drakkar cinema?

JANINE: (*Delighted*) Behind the town hall, the Drakkar cinema, seven, seven thirty, that's easy to remember!

(*In conclusion, he offers her his hand.*)

MICHEL: Good night.

JANINE: (*Taking it warmly*) Good night.

(*She gets out of the car. He leans out.*)

MICHEL: Janine! I'm so glad I met you!

JANINE: Thanks. Me too, very. So, see you tomorrow, then?

(MICHEL *seems happy and worried at the same time.*)

MICHEL: Yes, tomorrow.

(*She makes for the imposing entrance to the bourgeois building,*

24

*pretends to ring the bell and waves 'goodbye' to the departing car,
which is soon out of sight. Then she quickly turns round the
corner, into the service entrance. Ecstatic.)*

SEVEN

Morning. A knock on the door.

LONGUET: Come in.
   *(The curtains are drawn; a lazy morning lie-in. An atmosphere of
   warmth and languor. Embarrassed,* JANINE *slips into the
   bedroom with the breakfast tray.)*
JANINE: Good morning, Monsieur. Good morning, Madame.
   *('Sir', 'Madam' – her employers look so young when they wake
   up in the morning. Longuet's hair is all mussed up.* SÉVERINE
   is asleep, or pretending to be. It's obvious that JANINE *is in the
   way. She points at the side table and murmurs:)*
   Shall I put it there?
LONGUET: No, on the bed, just here. Thank you, Janine.
   *(She tiptoes over, blushing, and puts the tray down. The bed's a
   mess. A protruding shoulder and the curve of a breast indicate
   that* SÉVERINE *must be naked under the sheets. On the night
   table, next to an open packet of Lucky Strikes, a cigarette is
   smouldering in the ashtray.
   Moments later,* JANINE *is ironing in the kitchen; she 'hears'
   their sighs and laughter.)*

   On the hills,
   On the hills,
   All powerful,
   All powerful . . .

(The final steps of a narrow staircase. JANINE *emerges on to the
mezzanine floor, guided by the sound of a rousing song, sung with
great emotion.)*

   All that can be heard,
   All that can be heard,
   Is the wind,

25

Is the wind . . .

(In the municipal hall, twenty choristers – men, women and children – are singing in full voice. MICHEL *is conducting them. Impressed,* JANINE *watches him discreetly, then she smiles, proudly. It's as though he's transformed, a different person: he's blossomed out of his shell. There's nothing left of yesterday's civil-servant type. At the harmonium, a woman with a gentle face, about thirty, is gazing ardently at* MICHEL. *Janine's sharp eyes immediately fasten upon a rival.*

A few moments later. JANINE *and* MICHEL *come out of the town hall, into the street.)*

JANINE: Is that your wife?

MICHEL: No, that's Lise.

JANINE: So is she your mistress?

(They go towards Michel's car, which is parked in a street next to a little park.)

MICHEL: Do you know who you remind me of? Esmeralda, the gypsy girl, in *The Hunchback of Notre Dame.*

JANINE: Who's she?

MICHEL: What! You've never read *The Hunchback of Notre Dame?* Abbot Frolo, the Court of Miracles, Quasimodo?

JANINE: Oh yes, I think I've seen the film with Quasimodo in it.

MICHEL: Good, but really you ought to read the book, you know. Victor Hugo is my favourite writer. He's a giant, a Titan among men! I do hope you like to read?

JANINE: *(Replying without too much enthusiasm)* Yes, of course.

MICHEL: And what about *Les Misérables?* Don't tell me you've never read *Les Misérables?*

JANINE: Well, I did read the beginning. I like beginnings best, because the endings – endings are often unhappy. *(With conviction)* But I'll read some Victor Hugo now.

MICHEL: Well, I hope so.

(She goes to open the door of the car. He forestalls her; there's a moment of confusion. She's not used to such consideration. They get into the car.)

JANINE: Tell me, why do I remind you of the gypsy girl? *(Already she's forgotten the name.)*

MICHEL: Esmeralda? Because you're like her, full of contrasts.

He was very big on contrasts, was Victor Hugo. You're frank and bold, unpredictable, shy and spontaneous. And I'm sure you're very passionate.
(*She takes one of his hands and examines it closely.*)
What are you doing?

JANINE: I'm reading the lines of your hand, since I'm a spontaneous gypsy girl. You know, you've got incredibly clean hands, and your fingernails are impeccable! (*She gives him back his hand.*)

MICHEL: (*Mischievously*) Well, I happen to know a beautician . . .
(JANINE *has obviously forgotten all about that.*)

JANINE: Oh, yes . . .
(MICHEL *offers her a small, flat package.*)

MICHEL: Here, this is for you.
(JANINE *looks at* MICHEL. *This is her first gift from a man. She unwraps the package.*)

JANINE: Is it a scarf?

MICHEL: (*Smiling*) Well, it isn't a bicycle.

JANINE: (*Radiant*) Oh, thank you.
(*She throws herself round his neck, rather fiercely, but it doesn't matter. They embrace, dramatically, as though their very lives depended on it. Then he slowly takes off his glasses and looks at her, and this time it's he who takes her in his arms and kisses her passionately.*)

MICHEL: Oh! This is madness.

JANINE: (*Taking hold of his hand and placing it on her chest*) My heart is really racing. Feel, can you feel it?

MICHEL: Yes, it's crazy.

JANINE: I've got small breasts, haven't I?

MICHEL: Yes . . . well, not too small.
(*They're off again! Kissing desperately, as though they were the last couple on earth. Then Janine gently disengages herself.*)

JANINE: You see, you do want to sleep with me.

MICHEL: (*Shaking his head, feeling terribly guilty*) I knew it was going to turn out like this! I just knew it! I thought I'd made my mind up, and now . . .

JANINE: Made your mind up about what?

MICHEL: About respecting you, of course.

JANINE: But I don't give a damn about your respect. Where does that get me? Nobody's asking you to respect me! Oh, I just don't understand any of it!

MICHEL: (*He seems nonplussed*) What I mean is, wanting something can sometimes be better than getting it. That 'before' is maybe better than 'after'.

JANINE: But 'before' means 'now' and 'now' is a pain. It's always the same old story!

MICHEL: Wait a minute. You're right. I'm just not explaining myself properly. Let me think.

JANINE: (*Exasperated*) No, *don't* think! Stop it! You're starting to get on my nerves, dammit! (*She throws the scarf in his face.*) Here, have it, I don't want it any more! Thanks for nothing! Thanks a lot! (*Angrily she gets out of the car, leaving Michel totally at a loss.*)

EIGHT

Someone's hammering away. Morning. JANINE *is changing the sheets in the Longuets' bedroom. From time to time she turns round, keeping an eye on the adjoining corridor. A young workman is putting up shelving. It's obvious she finds him attractive. He seems to have similar feelings about her, but he's shy. He smiles at her a few times, vaguely, then goes back to work, while she attends to hers.* SÉVERINE LONGUET *calls to* JANINE *from the hall.*)

SÉVERINE: Janine? I'm going out.

JANINE: Yes, Madame.

(*Before leaving the bedroom,* JANINE *gives one last little look at the young workman. He glances back at her. Then, the sound of his hammer. In the hall.* SÉVERINE LONGUET *is getting ready to go out.*)

What time will you be back, Madame?

SÉVERINE: Twelve. Twelve thirty at the latest. Goodbye, Janine.

(*Hammering can be heard at the back of the apartment. As* JANINE *goes back towards the room,* SÉVERINE *comes back in. A false exit. In the half-open doorway,* SÉVERINE *glances towards the bedroom.*)

28

Look, keep a discreet eye on him. These workers are decent people, but you never know.

JANINE: Yes, Madame.

(*The door closes again.* JANINE *makes a beeline for the bedroom. Tap, tap! Sound of the hammer at work. In the corridor, the young workman is still secretly watching her. She approaches the bed, takes up an armful of big soft pillows, goes towards a small table and – accidentally on purpose? – knocks over some ornaments on it. The young workman rushes to help, crouching down to pick up the pieces, then gently but firmly takes her wrist in his hand.*

Reading by candlelight. We can see . . .

'*I'm no longer a v . . . she tearfully confessed to him. She was deeply distressed, but at the same time full of inexpressible happiness.*'

Douce Étoile, *a slim novel with an illustrated cover, joins* Troublante Chimère *and* The Film Annual *on the bedside table in the maid's attic room.* JANINE *blows her candle out. Darkness.*

A bookshop. A long, double shelf of Pléiade classics, all of them by Victor Hugo. Janine's hand is seen deftly swiping one of the books. There's a sensual quality to her swift, skilful movements. The book is slid out of its cardboard case and its white dustjacket is removed. It is slipped, minus its dustjacket, into her handbag. The white dustjacket, now 'empty', is put back into the cardboard case, which is then returned to its place on the shelf. What she puts back is indeed a true work of fiction. Tring! The shop door rings as it is opened, then closed again.

Shadow and sunlight. Sitting against the wall of a covered alleyway in the town centre, Janine scrawls on the frontispiece of the stolen book:

'*I am no longer a v*
So there's no reason to delay.')

NINE

Residential suburb. Greenery. We're looking through the windscreen of Michel's car. JANINE *is wearing a pretty summer dress. She can't suppress her excitement.*

JANINE: But you're not telling it right! Tell me all the details! What exactly did you say to her?

MICHEL: Well, just what I told you: my best friend was in a car accident, he was in a critical condition in hospital and he was asking for me!

JANINE: So?

MICHEL: So, I'm not feeling very proud of myself right now.

JANINE: You're right. It's not a very good lie. Did your wife believe you?

MICHEL: (*Uneasy*) I hope so. It's so awful, what I told her – something that awful could only be true. Look, we're there. (*A pleasant secluded little hotel. Rather more than* MICHEL *can afford. At the counter in the hall, a* RECEPTIONIST, *crabby and 'of a certain age', looks up from the register and looks at the couple who have just come in.*)

MICHEL: Good day, Mademoiselle. I would like two rooms, please, one for me and one for my daughter. (JANINE *waits, hanging back a little, her suitcase at her feet. The* RECEPTIONIST *is suspicious.*)

RECEPTIONIST: A small or a large bed?

MICHEL: (*Hesitating, then*) A medium-sized bed will do fine. Thank you, mademoiselle. (*The staircase which leads to the rooms.*)

JANINE: (*Whispering to* MICHEL) Why do you call her 'Mademoiselle?' She must be over a hundred!

MICHEL: (*Whispering back*) You should always address employees as 'Mademoiselle'. (*They join the* RECEPTIONIST, *who is standing between two doors.*)

RECEPTIONIST: Number 18 for Monsieur. Number 19 for the young lady.

(JANINE *disappears into her room.*)

MICHEL: Thank you. Thank you very much. Good night, Mademoiselle.

(*Bewildered, the* RECEPTIONIST *moves away towards the stairs, looking at her watch.*)

RECEPTIONIST: Good night?

(*It's still broad daylight.*

A little later, then JANINE *comes furtively out of her room and scratches at Michel's door. He opens it hurriedly.*)

JANINE: (*With a broad smile*) Should I come to you, or you to me?

MICHEL: I've really no idea.

JANINE: Well, let's say it should be me. (*She slips into his room.*)

(*Later. Outside the open window a tree rustles. The room is simple and well aired. Their clothes are strewn about the floor.* MICHEL *and* JANINE *have been making love. They're asleep now, Janine's slender, childlike arm around Michel's body. She's the one to wake first; she's careful not to disturb him. She looks at the stranger sleeping beside her.*

Later. His turn to wake up. She's tied her hair up and is wearing Michel's shirt. Curled up in an armchair, she's going through the contents of his wallet.)

MICHEL: So you're going through my pockets now?

JANINE: (*Playful*) Yes. I've a right to know everything about your life now! (*She laughs. She's just come across the photo on his identity papers.*) Oh, but you're so ugly here!

(*She jumps on to the bed with him. He wraps his arms around her. She rests her face against his chest.*)

We're the happiest pair on earth, aren't we?

(*He seems to feel exactly the same way.*)

Well, do you want me to tell you who I did it with that first time?

MICHEL: No! Certainly not!

JANINE: Why 'certainly not!'?

MICHEL: Because that should stay a secret. It belongs to you; it's something precious.

JANINE: (*Pulling a cheeky face*) Huh . . . talk about something precious! That's nothing precious about it at all! You don't

31

go around wanting to lose something precious!

MICHEL: You were so . . . You seemed in such a hurry . . .

JANINE: (*Looking pleased with herself*) Yes, I was sure it'd be really great.

MICHEL: Really? You didn't find it in any way disgusting?

JANINE: Yeah, really disgusting! And then, fantastic! You can show how much you love each other without having to say a word. (*She gets up and smiles at him, the enchanting smile of a happy child. Mewing behind the door.* JANINE *half opens it. On the threshold, a little kitten looks up at her.*) Wait. (*She sneaks into the corridor, bare-legged and still in his shirt, takes what's left of tea and milk from a tray in front of someone else's door and brings it back for the kitten, who laps it all up immediately.*) Come on, little fellow, drink it all up. (*She goes back into the room.*)

MICHEL: How do you know it's a boy?

JANINE: Men always make a fuss about getting what they want. (*She looks at herself in the vanity mirror, pulling on 'her' shirt-tails.*) Don't you think it suits me? You don't mind me wearing it?

MICHEL: Well, I mind a bit, yes.

JANINE: Why?

MICHEL: Because it'll smell of your perfume.

JANINE: (*Mildly irritated*) Well, excuse me! Do you want me to take it off?

MICHEL: Of course not.

(*Downcast, she stops moving around, takes the Hugo classic from the dressing table and comes back to sit on the bed next to* MICHEL, *flicking through the pages with her back turned to him.*)

JANINE: (*Muttering miserably*) I don't know, all this poetry . . .

MICHEL: Yes?

JANINE: Isn't it a bit boring?

(*She turns round to see if he's responding to her provocation. Stony silence.*)

Are you sulking?

MICHEL: I'm thinking.

(*Silence.*)

It's just you're so young. You're really no more than a young girl.

32

JANINE: You've figured that out all by yourself, have you – that I'm a young girl? Anyway, I'm not a young girl any more – you should be calling me a 'young woman'. I'm an adult. No one's got the right to have a go or punish me any more. (*At the thought of this, her good humour returns.*) I'm fed up with everyone having a go all the time! And another thing – we should stop lying to each other.

MICHEL: Why d'you say that?

JANINE: Because I've told some terrible lies.

MICHEL: Such as?

JANINE: Well, like saying I'm a beautician.

MICHEL: And you're not?

JANINE: No, nothing like. I'm a maid, a housemaid, and I don't live at 11, avenue du Parc – well, not exactly. I've got an attic room in the building.

MICHEL: (*Nodding: it's all clear to him now*) So you mean you've got a maid's room in the building?

JANINE: Yes, that's it. (*Suddenly upset.*) But you'll still come and see me, won't you? It's on the top floor, I warn you. There's an awful lot of stairs!

(MICHEL *smiles at her.*)

You're not annoyed with me, then?

MICHEL: Of course not. (*He gets up and grabs his trousers.*)

JANINE: So why are you getting dressed?

MICHEL: I'm getting dressed because it's time to get dressed. How is it you can afford classic editions of Victor Hugo on a maid's wages?

JANINE: (*Looking at him before blurting out*) I didn't buy it, I stole it.

MICHEL: (*Adjusting his trousers; he's very calm*) Is that why there was no cover on it?

JANINE: That's why.

MICHEL: Could I have my shirt back, now, if you don't mind?

JANINE: I can see you're really sulking now. (*She takes off his shirt and holds it out to him.*)

MICHEL: I'm not sulking, it's just that it's such a shame. I brought the book along so I could read some of it to you and now . . .

JANINE: And now you don't feel like it?

33

MICHEL: Well, let's say I'm upset.

JANINE: But if I lied and I stole, it was all for you. It was to make you feel good.

(*Sits on the bed, utterly crushed; impossible to make her out. Not knowing what to do, he joins her and puts his arm around her shoulders. She mutters darkly*) It wasn't worth sleeping together. You don't treat me like a grown-up.

MICHEL: Yes, I do. Look, I'll make you a deal. I'll make an effort if you promise not to steal any more, not even a book.

JANINE: (*Getting her own back*) So how am I supposed to get you a present like that on my wages?

MICHEL: You've got a point there. (*He thinks for a moment.*) How far did you get in school?

JANINE: (*Not keen on this turn in the conversation*) School cert.

MICHEL: Did you pass?

JANINE: I left.

MICHEL: Why?

JANINE: I can't remember any more.

MICHEL: And how did you do in composition?

(*Janine looks at him blankly. He explains gently.*)

MICHEL: Essay writing.

JANINE: Sometimes all right, sometimes not. (*She smiles.*) It's true! Depending on the subject.

MICHEL: Okay, I get it. One: You haven't really got a proper job. Two: you need to improve your education. I'm going to take you in charge. I'll find you something suitable, you'll see.

TEN

A sign above the entrance to a courtyard:

'Pigier. Secretarial courses. Shorthand, typing lessons, etc.'

MICHEL *comes out of the building, carrying a bunch of brochures.* JANINE *waits for him in the car, eating an ice-cream wafer. He gets in beside her and opens a brochure.*

MICHEL: Look, that's a typewriter keyboard. Impressive, isn't it? You should use it to write all your love letters.

(*A few days later.* JANINE *is at her first typing lesson at Pigier's. She hesitates over the keys. She makes awkward attempts at the shorthand symbols, tears the page up and starts again. Then she starts to tap at the keyboard, faster this time.*

At work at the Longuets'. Perched on a stool, she cleans the windows; she buffs the parquet flooring with steel wool. The service stairway which goes up to Janine's attic room. The concierge is in the corridor with her bucket and mop. She disappears. MICHEL *emerges from the corner where he's been lurking, his arms full of books. He stops in front of Janine's door, which is wide open. She's in the middle of a big clean-up, in his honour. She turns round, sees him and smiles her smile for special occasions . . . He comes into the room. She throws her arms round his neck, standing on tiptoe.*

Pigier's. A busy hum now fills the room, which is vibrating with the noise. JANINE *is pluckily typing away. Tired, however (all this extra work), she smothers a yawn, then goes to it again, clenching her teeth.*

A row in the dress circle at the municipal theatre. The concert has begun. MICHEL *is late, disturbing those already seated. The usual whispered apologies.*)

MICHEL: Excuse me, excuse me. Good evening, Madame Garraut, excuse me.

MADAME GARRAUT: Don't mention it, Monsieur Davenne. (*In these provincial towns, everyone knows everyone else. He arrives at Janine's seat and points to the place next to her.*)

MICHEL: Excuse me, Mademoiselle, is this seat taken?

JANINE: I was waiting for a friend, Monsieur, but I don't think she's coming now.

MICHEL: May I?

JANINE: You may.

(*The delight of their private play-acting.* MICHEL *sits down. In the darkness, their hands touch. The music grows louder.*)

35

The Longuets' bedroom.

SÉVERINE: And if you see me reach for a cigarette, you're to
say, 'No, Madame'. You will, won't you?
(SÉVERINE *emerges from her dressing room, carrying an armful
of clothes; five months' pregnant, her stomach is large and round.
Behind the screen,* JANINE *is trying on some underwear.*
SÉVERINE *runs a critical eye over her clothes as she throws one
garment after another on to the armchair.*)

SÉVERINE: That's something I won't be wearing again . . . that
one . . . (*She hesitates*) That one I might be able to wear
again, but not for months . . . then, that one, well, you might
as well have that too.
(JANINE'*s face emerges, curious, over the top of the screen to
have a look.*)

SÉVERINE: Look at that? What on earth was I doing buying
that! I must have been mad! (*She babbles on, gaily.*) No
self-respecting mother wears satin, it's not decent!

(*Charming and simple,* JANINE *comes out from behind the screen in a silk 'teddy'. Her long legs. Her natural grace. Instinctively she turns to look at herself in the mirror.* SÉVERINE *looks at her, taken aback. It's like a scene in a film by Jean Renoir: there's little age difference between the two women, simply a difference of circumstances. Dressed as she is,* JANINE *has as much class and charm as her employer.*)

SÉVERINE: Well, I'll say, you're going to drive the men crazy! (*A pause, then, with curiosity:*) Have you got a boyfriend? (*Looking at herself three-quarters on, to assess the effect,* JANINE *nods.*)

JANINE: Mmm . . . mmm . . .

SÉVERINE: (*Amused*) You're starting early. Is he the same age as you? (*She offers her another garment.* JANINE *goes back behind the screen.*)

JANINE: Oh, no. Boys my age are, well, you know! My boyfriend is forty-three, actually.

SÉVERINE: Ah, an older man! And what does he do?

JANINE: I don't know. He's a musician in the Land Registry. Something like that.

SÉVERINE: A musician? That's not bad!

JANINE: Not that wonderful either. He's got problems with his wife. She doesn't like classical music. Sometimes he has to go to the cinema by himself.

SÉVERINE: (*Shocked but intrigued*) A married man? Well done! (*They laugh.* JANINE *comes out from behind the screen in a 'Mademoiselle Swing' dress.*)

JANINE: Are you pleased about having a baby?

SÉVERINE: (*Placing her hands on her belly*) Very. Doesn't it show, how happy I am? But it's also quite scary, of course: labour and all that. I'm frightened of how much it will hurt.

JANINE: (*Horrified*) You think it's going to be really painful, then?

SÉVERINE: Of course. You ought to be careful with your 'lover', you know. It's very easily done, getting pregnant, as easy as catching a cold. And once it's happened, with a lot of men, that's the last you see of them. (*Disheartened,* JANINE *flops into an armchair.*)

37

There are precautions you can take. I'll give you some things to read. This child was wanted, planned for. Do you know anything about the 'Ogino Method'?

(*No,* JANINE *has never heard of it.* SÉVERINE *finds a* Cinemonde *magazine and flicks through the ads in it.*)

Wait, here we are. Look, read this.

(*They look at the magazine, heads close together. The cavernous voice of Dr Ogino is heard:*

LADIES! you should be aware of the fact that a woman is only fertile on certain days of the month! bla bla bla . . . bla bla bla . . .

The attic room. Janine's hand is seen picking up her elastic hairband from the bedside table on which The Hunchback of Notre Dame *and* 93 *have taken the place of* Tendre Tourment *and* The Film Annual *. . . On the bed,* JANINE *fixes her hair.*)

JANINE: What would you do if I was pregnant?

(MICHEL, *in the middle of tying his shoelaces, stops short. He is amazed.*)

MICHEL: Are you late?

JANINE: A bit.

MICHEL: How late? (*He's gone pale. Silence. She lets him stew.*)

JANINE: Oh, you should see your face! No, I'm not late. I'm as regular as the seasons.

MICHEL: (*Extremely annoyed*) First of all, the expression is 'regular as clockwork', not 'regular as the seasons'. 'I'm regular as clockwork' is what you say. Secondly, I find it appalling that you should joke about such things!

JANINE: But I'm not joking. I'm lying. I warned you what a good liar I was. (*Silence, then pensively:*) My father, as soon as he knew my mother was pregnant, he dumped her like an old pair of shoes . . . and . . .

MICHEL: And?

JANINE: (*Enigmatically*) That's the last that was seen of him.

MICHEL: Yes, but what's your father got to do with me? Your father, your father, why do you always have to compare him with me? He doesn't sound up to much, your father! I wouldn't behave anything like your father!

JANINE: Quite. That's exactly what I'm asking you. How would you behave?

MICHEL: Well, I don't know. If you were going to have a child by me, it would be serious, really serious. I'd have to . . . have to . . .

JANINE: You'd have to 'think it over', I suppose.

MICHEL: Well, yes.

TWELVE

In front of the Pigier building, a group of students standing around; then they disperse, looking annoyed. JANINE, *who's just got there, questions one of her classmates.*

JANINE: What's happening?

CLASSMATE: There are workmen up there. They're repairing the roof.

JANINE: So?

CLASSMATE: So, there's no class today.

JANINE: (*Angry*) They could have told us! I've left my notebooks up there, and I've got a lot of catching up to do! I've got to go up there!

CLASSMATE: But it's all locked up. How are you going to get in?

JANINE: Don't worry, I'll manage. See you later!

(*The Pigier landing, on the top floor. Using her nail-file,* JANINE *picks the lock in a matter of seconds. Without a sound, she slips in to the deserted classroom and picks up her notebooks from her desk. Suddenly she hears a muffled sound. It's coming from the end of the corridor, from the office marked 'Administration'. The door is half open. Intrigued, she approaches stealthily, to take a look. In the office, a young man (about eighteen or nineteen) dressed in a workman's overall, is going through a box file. On the table is what he's found already: envelopes stuffed with little bundles of banknotes. On one of them can be read: 'Janine Castang – course fees'. She makes a sudden entrance.*)

Don't mind me!

YOUNG THIEF: (*Jumping as though he's had an electric shock*) Hello, Mademoiselle. Look, I'll put everything back and you needn't say a word. It's like you dreamed it. You didn't see me, OK?

39

(*Just at this moment, the penetrating voice of the* SCHOOL DIRECTOR, *a woman, is heard from the stairs.*)

DIRECTOR: But this is a ridiculous state of affairs! You are the concierge, I am the head of the school! I'm all for the roof being repaired, but I could have been informed, all the same. It's a bit much, isn't it?

(*A moment of stupefaction. Then the* THIEF *makes a leap for the skylight window – presumably, his means of entry. But it's not quite as easy as it was getting in. He tries, clinging to the window frame, feet treading air. He doesn't look particularly menacing. Meanwhile,* JANINE *deftly rearranges the envelopes in their box. He can't make it and has to climb down, annoyed and helpless. The* DIRECTOR *appears.*)

DIRECTOR: What on earth are you doing here, Janine? And you, young man?

(*She goes immediately to check whether there's anything missing from the box of envelopes. Relief. As for* JANINE, *for once it's not her who's the thief. She can play the innocent. With just the right amount of fear and assumed contrition, she speaks.*)

JANINE: I came up to get my books so I could work at home. And as the door wasn't locked . . .

DIRECTOR: What? It wasn't locked?

JANINE: No, that's how I could come in. I was just about to go downstairs and tell the concierge when I heard a noise. So I came to have a look. But it wasn't anything, just the window which was open and the man here who was working on the roof.

(*As always,* JANINE *is a good liar. Feeling more confident, and somewhat amused, the young man chips in.*)

YOUNG THIEF: She's afraid to tell you that as I was trying to chat her up, I took the liberty of coming in.

(*The* DIRECTOR *looks utterly confused.*)

JANINE: (*As if butter wouldn't melt . . .*) But we weren't doing anything wrong. We were going to . . .

YOUNG THIEF: We 'were going to' but we didn't!

DIRECTOR: (*Looking at the pair of them severely*) This is all very confusing! Neither of you have any business being here. (*To* JANINE) Go home and get on with some work. (*To the youth:*) And you can get on with yours.

(*He doesn't need telling twice. He clambers on to a chair and hoists himself up through the window, though not before a polite farewell.*)

YOUNG THIEF: Madame, mademoiselle.

(*The* YOUNG THIEF *catches up with* JANINE *in the street.*)

YOUNG THIEF: Hey, I didn't get round to saying thank you.

JANINE: Well, you can say it now!

YOUNG THIEF: Thank you, Janine. I'm Raoul. Why didn't you give me away?

JANINE: Because I'm not a sneak. How about you? Are you a workman or a thief?

RAOUL: Both, but I'm thinking of dropping the workman bit. (*He looks into her eyes. He has that rather sudden brashness often found in shy people, and a strange way of walking. His hair is slicked down at the back. His workman's toolbag is stained with greasy food spots.*) Where are you going?

JANINE: Why?

RAOUL: Because I'm going that way myself.

JANINE: Oh really? You're pushing your luck, aren't you?

RAOUL: You're right, and d'you know why? It's because of the bombing at Liberation. I was still at school but I wasn't doing very well. One day I got my school report and I'd come bottom of the class. I was scared of getting told off, so I didn't go home, which was all for the best 'cos a bomb dropped on it. So ever since I've been pushing my luck.

JANINE: And what about your parents? Are they dead?

RAOUL: They never found them. I'm living at the Catholic Youth Workers. You get bed and board, but the priest can't stand me. I don't think I'm going to stay there much longer. Let's have a look over there.

(*He leads her over to a stall with a display of cheap goods. A job lot of sunglasses.* RAOUL *examines them whilst whistling absently the tune to 'A Little Night Music'. He seems really taken with the sunglasses.* JANINE *catches the look in his eyes. Then she points to a spot down the road.*)

JANINE: You know, I fancy an ice-cream sundae in the café over there.

RAOUL: (*Looking along the road, hands shading his eyes*) Bar des Sportifs? I know it. But I better tell you right now, I'm flat broke. Haven't even got enough for a beer, or a pair of sunglasses.

JANINE: Don't worry, it's my treat.

(*On the way there. It's not far. He has an impulse to put his arm round Janine's shoulders.*)

RAOUL: Can we say 'tu' to each other?

JANINE: OK.

(*She deftly removes his hand. He laughs, and starts whistling: 'A Little Night Music'.*

In front of the Bar des Sportifs, there's a sign posted up: 'Moto-cross Tournament'. Reigning champions Schmidt and Vasseur are announced as taking part.)

RAOUL: Schmidt's the one who'll win! Vasseur really gives his machine a lot of punishment. But if Schmidt's going to be there, it's hardly worth bothering. (*He turns round, realizing he's talking into thin air.*) Where's she gone?

(*JANINE has disappeared. He's disappointed. No, here she is again.*)

JANINE: I got a ladder in my stocking. Had to fix it.

RAOUL: And there I was, thinking you'd dumped me.

(*They sit down on the terrace.*)

Do you like moto-cross?

JANINE: I don't know. I've never been.

RAOUL: I'll take you one day, if you like. Sometimes I compete but at the moment . . . if you could see the bike I've got, it's a 'Terrot' with a side car, you'd see the problems I've got with it. I'd be coming off the track and crashing all the time. (*Suddenly enthusiastic.*) Look, look over there! can you see Cohen's team? (*He points to the wasteground opposite, where a half-dozen bikes are careering around the slopes of the moto-cross course.*) They're the real bikers! They've agreed I can go as part of the team, but you have to have your own bike. That's why I need some money. A really good machine, an English make – even secondhand, I could do it up. I could really get some speed up, win a lot of rallies. Then I'd really be somebody. (*To impress the young girl at his side, he tries tapping his cigarette pack on the back of his hand and flicking a cigarette out to catch it in his mouth, but misses.*)

Damn! Look, are you going to get into trouble at the school because of me? I suppose you must be mad at me?

(*She doesn't reply. She takes out of her bag the pair of sunglasses he'd had his eye on, and puts them on the table before him.*) What's this, then?

JANINE: Proof I'm not mad at you.

(*A pause, then he picks up the glasses and examines them.*)

RAOUL: OK. I'll take them. That's really nice of you. But promise me you'll let me pay you back.

JANINE: (*Shaking her head*) You couldn't ever 'pay' me back.

RAOUL: Why not?

JANINE: Because I didn't pay for them.

(*As she says this, she gives him one of her sunniest smiles. OK. They're two of a kind.* RAOUL *is completely won over.*)

RAOUL: I've got my bike back over there. If you want, I could take you for a ride.

(JANINE *is flattered and she'd love to, but . . .*)

JANINE: I can't. I've got to get dinner ready for my employers. (*A pause.*)

RAOUL: You're not working as a maid, are you? (*He seems put out, disappointed.*) It's so stupid, being a maid.

JANINE: I know. That's why I'm doing the course at Pigier's. So I can do shorthand and typing, be a secretary.

RAOUL: That's even worse!

JANINE: Why?

RAOUL: (*Leaning over with a schoolmasterly air*) Look, I'll explain it to you. Right now, you're a maid, you're working for two people, but when you're a secretary, you'll be working for maybe a hundred, a thousand people. It depends on how big the company is. Get it? Honestly, you're better off as a maid . . . (JANINE *seems shaken. As for* RAOUL, *he's gone off into a daydream.*)

Still, there are some compensations to being a maid. Take my sister Simone: before the war, she was a maid for some incredibly rich people. They were so rich they had a Van Gogh in the living room. Do you know what a Van Gogh is? Well, believe me, it's worth a lot of money. Anyway, guess what she found behind the painting one day? A safe! And you know what? The Van Gogh was a fake.

(*What!* JANINE *is devastated.*)
But the safe turned out to be genuine, all right. No doubt about it!
(*The next day, at the Longuets,* JANINE *is dusting and whistling Raoul's tune ('A Little Night Music') and ogling the pictures on the walls. On the off-chance, she lifts one away from the wall. Nothing!*

The hallway. The doorbell rings. Insistently. JANINE *runs to open it. It's* LONGUET, *pale and dishevelled. He's supporting* SÉVERINE, *who looks terrible.*)

LONGUET: Quickly, Janine! Come and help her.
(*As he rushes over to the telephone,* JANINE *helps* SÉVERINE *on to the settee in the living room.*)
(*On the phone*) Hello, Jean, where on earth have you been? Séverine's having a miscarriage! But of course it's an 'accident'! What? We were at the cinema. Yes. She's in terrible pain. Yes, but hurry up!
(*On the settee,* SÉVERINE *is sweating profusely, short of breath, desperate.*)

SÉVERINE: I'm going to lose my baby, Janine.
(*JANINE pats her mistress's hand. She doesn't know what to say or do.*)

44

JANINE: Don't worry. I'll give you the clothes back if it makes
you feel any better.
(*Then she falls silent, cowed by* SÉVERINE's *terrifying pain and
emotional suffering.*)

THIRTEEN

A country road. RAOUL *and* JANINE *are on the 'Terrot', intoxicated
with speed, with youth. It's one of those wonderful days you remember
for the rest of your life.* JANINE *is very fetching in the side-car. With
her leather cap, she looks like a young pioneer aviator.*

*A bustling, jolly terrace dance-café on the riverside. There are families
taking aperitifs. It's obviously a Sunday. There are couples dancing a
waltz, a beautiful whirling dance.*

With their ice-cream sundaes in front of them, JANINE *and* RAOUL
*are laughing and whispering. They're getting on like a house on fire,
clowning around.* RAOUL *is trying to impress her with his sleight-of-
hand tricks. Crash! He breaks his glass and the carafe. They run off,
giggling like a pair of kids ringing doorbells.*

*They're walking down the street together, closely entwined. We can't
hear exactly what* RAOUL *is saying to* JANINE. *Whatever it is, his
tender words seem desperately sincere. Suddenly he stops and hugs*
JANINE *close to him. A couple of kids, in love, amid the crowd of
passers-by.*

*Later. A cellar, full of broken-down slot machines, a job-lot of record
players, old records. The young couple are trying to make love right
there on the floor, on a pile of old sheet-music.* RAOUL *is rather
awkward. Covered in sweat, he finally gives up and rolls over on his
side, his forehead buried in his arm.*

JANINE: (*Murmuring gently*) It doesn't matter. They say that
when you really love each other, it doesn't work the first time
anyway.
RAOUL: Well, then, I must really love you a lot. (*Silence. He
looks at her, and then, sincerely:*) It's true, you know! Anyway,
I have to be in bed to get it right. (*Gesturing:*) We need

45

proper sheets! (*Suddenly he raises himself on one elbow.*) Hey, look over there! Record players!

(*Janine's room, an hour later. On the floor, next to their shoes, one of the record players which they must have pinched. In bed.* RAOUL *manages to carry off the cigarette routine, catching it in his mouth after tapping it out of the packet on the back of his hand.* JANINE *passes him the candle for a light. He blows the smoke affectedly towards the ceiling, like a character from a Peter Cheyney novel. He looks at her with a warm smile on his face. Like hers. It's clear it was a lot better this time round. Then he gets up, crouches down next to the record player, fiddles with the dials, shakes the pick-up arm.*)

JANINE: (*In bed*) You know, those things work better when they're plugged in!

RAOUL: You're right! Damn it! What a dump! (*He's as thin as a rake in his enormous white underpants. Hands on hips, he looks dreamily round the room.*) Mind you, it'd make a good hiding place for the rooty-toot-toot (*he mimes a pickpocket*), wouldn't it?

JANINE: Rooty-toot-toot?

RAOUL: Yes, the rooty-toot-toot. Don't you know what that means? What does it rhyme with . . . begins with l?

JANINE: (*She's got it and is vastly amused.*) Loot! Rooty-toot-toot!

RAOUL: There you are! Rhyming slang . . . Get it?

FOURTEEN

In town. A traffic cop blows his whistle. Stop. At a gesture from the white baton, Michel's car pulls up next to another car with two women in the front seats. MICHEL *suddenly notices them and ducks down. Bent under the steering wheel, he mutters.*

MICHEL: Christ! It's my wife!

(*Next to him,* JANINE *is thrilled.*)

JANINE: Will they recognize your car?

MICHEL: There's a good chance they might.

(*No danger. The two women are too absorbed in conversation.*)

JANINE: (*Intensely curious*) Which one is she? The one who's driving?

MICHEL: (*In a whisper*) No, the other one.

JANINE: (*Amazed*) Gosh! She's really good-looking!

(*It's true. Michel's wife, in the car next to them, is very attractive. The cop signals for the traffic to start moving again.* MICHEL *takes care to allow the car next to them to go in front.*)

JANINE: (*Sarcastically*) You were terrified!

(*The attic room. A jumble of disparate objects; Janine's and Raoul's most recent pickings. Sitting on the bed,* JANINE *whistles 'A Little Night Music' as she applies nail varnish to her toes. As he reaches for his tie, looped over the arm of a bronze statuette of Mercury,* MICHEL *almost knocks over some bottles of wine on the mantelpiece.*)

JANINE: Careful!

MICHEL: (*Examining the bottles*) Pommard 1938, huh! Your

47

employers must think they're living in the House of Rothschild!

JANINE: What's the House of Rothschild?

MICHEL: It means they're acting like Lord and Lady Muck, using your room as an extra wine-cellar!

JANINE: (*Captivated*) I could tell them they're Lord and Lady Muck!

MICHEL: (*Fixing his tie*) Quite! You're done for if you let them take advantage. You've got your rights, you know!

(*Suddenly, there's a knock at the door. Five light taps! Michel's look of surprise. From the other side of the door, RAOUL, a 'work of art' on his shoulder – like Jean Gabin in* Les Bas-Fonds – *is whistling 'A Little Night Music', the signal to let her know it's him. Inside the room,* JANINE *and* MICHEL *go rigid. The hands that were tying his tie are frozen in mid-air; sitting on the bed, she holds the nail-varnish brush suspended . . .* MICHEL *has realized. She realizes he's realized.* RAOUL's *behind the door. His whistling continues, with trills, variations – becomes quite a serenade. Then, silence. Like a film which starts again after stopping on a freeze-frame,* MICHEL *goes on fixing his tie,* JANINE *finishes off her toe-nails. Leaden silence. But she watches him from the corner of her eye, looking for a reaction which doesn't come. Finally, with false calm, he speaks.*)

Well, what do I mean to you, exactly? Five hours a week?

JANINE: Four.

MICHEL: Yes. But it's not really quite enough for you, is it? (*He grabs his jacket from the back of a chair and hurriedly puts it on.*)

JANINE: But he's a boy. He's like me, don't you understand? What I mean is, he's had the same kind of life as me, pretty awful. And he doesn't want me to keep on with the Pigier course. He says it's stupid being a maid! (*Continuing*) And it's even more stupid being a skivvy for a whole lot of people, in a factory! And that's what being a secretary is! Stupid, stupid, stupid!

MICHEL: (*Managing to hide his discomfiture*) Yes, I see. He's a great guy and you're in love with him, is that it?

JANINE: How should I know? (*She gets out the photo-booth photos she's slipped into a book as a marker, a strip of six snaps, herself and* RAOUL – *a display of hilarious and monstrous face-pulling.*)

MICHEL: (*Bruised*) Oh yes, too funny for words.

FIFTEEN

One evening. Surprise. Emotion. On the pavement outside Pigier's,
UNCLE ROULEAU! *He's watching for* JANINE *coming out;*
awkward in his Sunday best, looking very old, holding a packet of
jellied fruits. The young girl sees him and runs up to him. They
embrace.

JANINE: What a surprise! I'm so happy to see you!

ROULEAU: (*Equally happy to see her*) Well, I went to your
employers first of all. Pretty posh area, isn't it? And the
mistress, a lovely woman, and ever so pleasant.

JANINE: Well, she can afford to be!

ROULEAU: She said I'd find you here, at the school. So you've
given up the bad old ways, then? You want to be a typist, is
that right?
(*She dodges the question. All dressed-up in her smart clothes, the
'kid' has certainly changed. He can't get over it.*)
Well, pet. You're turning into a right little beauty. Except
for your nose. No change there. Still looks like a gherkin.
(*A tea-room. Not the poshest, but quite imposing all the same.*
JANINE *wants to impress her uncle. She does. An elderly*
waitress with a little trolley. Tea for JANINE. *White coffee for*
him. A discreet gasp of pleasure at the pastries. Such gluttony.)

JANINE: (*In a worldly tone, whilst they're being served*) I just love
coming here! It's not too fancy, but quite excellent. Thank
you, Mademoiselle.
(*A look of surprise from* ROULEAU: *'Mademoiselle'.*)

ROULEAU: (*Bumbling like an old man*) Where's the milk?

JANINE: There, look. Don't bother, I'll take care of it. (*She
attends to him delicately. She enjoys looking after him.*) Has
Mum not written?
(*Silence. He tries to distract her, pointing at the enormous piece of
cake she's taking.*)

ROULEAU: You chose the biggest one!

JANINE: (*Lost in thought*) Yes.

ROULEAU: What're you thinking about?

JANINE: Nothing. D'you remember when Mum used to come and pick me up from the nursery in the boulevard Aristide-Briand, before the war, she used to take me to the pink cake-shop?

ROULEAU: Yes, you were five years old and you looked like a tadpole.

JANINE: She used to love that, watching me choose the cakes. I used to take ages deciding, and in the end I always used to choose the biggest one, even if it wasn't my favourite kind. (*She smiles. But her smile disappears abruptly as she sinks into mournful reverie. Silence.*)

ROULEAU: How stupid of me – I nearly forgot. (*He takes out a page from a drawing pad and holds it out to her.*) Have a look at this.

(*A portrait of* JANINE. *Quite well done.*)

And for that one I didn't use the pantograph, you know. I did it all from memory!

JANINE: It's pretty good. So don't you use your little gadget any more?

ROULEAU: You must be joking! Thank goodness I've still got it! 'Cos ever since Pascouette walked out on your aunt, I can tell you, it's not much fun around the house!

JANINE: What, isn't he going with Léa any more?

ROULEAU: No. (*Silence. He nods sorrowfully, as if it were a conspiracy against him.*) D'you remember the chrysanthemums? That bastard Pascouette was supposed to split the profits with your aunt! Well, she ended up with bugger all! After All Saints', he pocketed the lot, and then, with no more than a bye-your-leave, off on his hols! So, as you can imagine, with your aunt being such a sentimental type, she went off on a binge – a long one – talk about out of her head! Obviously, it hasn't improved her temper, but I suppose I'm used to it, and anyway, that's not the worst.

JANINE: And what's that?

ROULEAU: Well, the other day she got really pie-eyed. She missed that awkward turning, next to the Ripeaus' house. She crashed into the postman, that daft bugger who's arsing about all the time. He's got a broken collar-bone. So he's not so daft now. He's really angry. He wants to make a formal complaint, since she was so sozzled she went and bit his finger!

JANINE: But what about Aunt Léa, was she OK?

ROULEAU: What do you think? She's like you, she's tough, but the van's a write-off!

JANINE: What about the stall in the market, then?

ROULEAU: Oh, that's all over and done with. You don't know the half of it! It's just not worth spending the money on repairs. No, I'm getting a job at the Maggi factory. It's not definite yet, though.

(*Silence.*)

JANINE: I've got a really nice job with the Longuets. If you could wait a couple of months, I could lend you a bit of money.

ROULEAU: That's not why I came to see you!

JANINE: I wasn't saying that.

(ROULEAU *grabs the bill. She tries to argue with him.*)

ROULEAU: Leave me be, can't you! (*He puts on his spectacles.*) So what does this little lot come to?

(*She looks at his thick, worn fingers fumbling in his tiny purse. They shake slightly.*

The choir. MICHEL *is conducting. From the balcony* JANINE *is watching him, amid a small group of other spectators. She takes a squint at the small portable harmonium Lise, the accompanist, is playing.*

A few days later. In the shop window of a secondhand dealer – the harmonium. Michel's car draws up in front of the shop. MICHEL *in the driving seat, looking grim . . .* JANINE *is sitting next to him.*)

MICHEL: I've talked to the shop owner. He told me a young girl sold it to him yesterday.

(*Silence.*)

JANINE: (*Gloomily*) Are you angry?

MICHEL: No.

JANINE: Yes you are. You won't look at me. That means you're angry.

MICHEL: I don't need to look at you. I'll remember your face as it is now, today, for the rest of my life.

(*Silence.*)

I suppose I just haven't spent enough time on you.

51

JANINE: Yes you have.

MICHEL: No. Not the way I should have. When you haven't done everything you possibly can for someone, you haven't really done anything at all. I haven't been able to do much for you.

JANINE: (*Truly bewildered; she mutters, almost inaudibly*) But you have done a lot for me.

MICHEL: The proof that I haven't is right here.

JANINE: You should give it another go . . .

MICHEL: I've lost confidence; I suppose I've just lost confidence in myself.

JANINE: So what are you planning to do?

MICHEL: Make a clean break.

JANINE: 'Make a clean break' means it's all over?

MICHEL: That's right. Yes, that's exactly what I mean. (*Silence.*)

JANINE: D'you want me to get out of the car now?

MICHEL: I don't mind.

(*He waits. She makes up her mind. He hears the door open, then close, quietly.* JANINE *walks away. He waits. Then he gets out of the car. The* SHOP-OWNER *is standing in the doorway of his shop – a big, bearded man who looks like a gypsy showman. Calmly he points in Janine's direction.*)

SHOP-OWNER: That's her, the girl I told you about.

(MICHEL *sees, for the last time, Janine's skirt as she turns the corner of the street.*

In her room, JANINE *slips some banknotes into a stamped envelope, addressed to: Monsieur André Rouleau . . . rue de la Redoute, Saint-Flovier . . . Deux-Sèvres'. On the table at which she's sitting as she does this, there's a mirror; reflected in it is* RAOUL, *completely naked, slipping quickly between the sheets.*)

SIXTEEN

Hellish uproar. A commentator is shouting. The moto-cross cauldron. Bikes scale the slopes and careen over into the puddles of water, showering the spectators, who shout encouragements to the racers. A little girl sitting on her father's shoulders claps enthusiastically. A shudder of excitement runs through the crowd. Only JANINE *is fed up; jostled about, with nothing to do.* RAOUL *is in trouble. His bike skids into the mud. He's thrown sprawling. Mud-spattered, he gets up and looks over to where his dream is fast disappearing: the winner, who's waving his bouquet of flowers and being kissed by a pretty girl. He indicates he's packing it in. That's all he needed!*

Near the track, a moment later.

JANINE: But at least you're still alive!

RAOUL: (*Angrily kicking the engine, which lies there like a beaten dog*) This bike is bloody useless! What a heap of shit!

JANINE: You could sell it!

RAOUL: Who to? To that fence who keeps ripping us off? We've never, ever, got a decent price for anything! We've never made any real money! It's pathetic!

JANINE: All right. So we're not too good at it.

RAOUL: What we need is a real break. Something big. D'you get me?

(*He looks at her. She gets his point.*

An empty street. JANINE *is on the look out for* RAOUL, *who stealthily slips out of an ancient, dilapidated building. He's carrying, on his shoulder, a moped with one wheel missing.*)

JANINE: Is that all you could find?

RAOUL: What if I told you it's half-way to a racing bike? Look here, the headlight's still working! (*He turns it on; a weak ray of light in the darkness.*) You could use this as a light in your room. So it's worth it just for that!

JANINE: No way! I don't want any more clutter in my room! Anyway, I've already told you, I don't want to take any more risks!

RAOUL: And then there's the bell! (*He twangs it; a ridiculous, mocking little sound.*) The bell still works. You're going to have a doorbell – pretty impressive, don't you think?

JANINE: (*Laughing*) Shut up, you! Stop teasing me.

(*He rings the bell. Tring! She thumps him affectionately. They disappear off into the night. Tring, tring.*

A little street in a small market town. JANINE *and* RAOUL *have pulled up on his bike in front of an antiques shop.* RAOUL *takes*

53

the tarpaulin cover off the side-car: various objects – what's left of their loot. A patronizing look from the ANTIQUE DEALER.)

ANTIQUE DEALER: It's repro stuff, isn't it?

RAOUL: (*Protesting*) No, M'sieur, it's an inheritance!

ANTIQUE DEALER: I don't take inheritance stuff. Did Le Gall send you?

RAOUL: (*Bluffing*) Yes . . .

ANTIQUE DEALER: (*Suddenly angry*) Well, in that case, no deal! D'you hear me? No way!

(*He disappears back into the shop.* JANINE *goes after him, as far as the doorway.*)

JANINE: (*Livid*) What a jerk! The bastard! (*She shouts so that he can hear.*) Fucking bastard!

RAOUL: Come on, forget it.

(*He starts up the side-car. He kicks furiously at the kick-start; the badly lubricated machinery stalls; it's got damp.* JANINE *is shivering with cold. Her nose is red. She's trying to keep herself warm, rubbing her arms – to no avail. Misery all round . . .*

One evening. The Longuets have guests. Laughter. The murmur of conversations throughout the apartment. In the hall, JANINE *takes the coats as the guests arrive. The bedroom serves as cloakroom. Piling up on the bed: ladies' handbags, coats, overcoats.*

JANINE *is having to work very hard: in the dining-room, it's hors-d'oeuvres to serve up, in the kitchen, it's put the roast in the oven, and in the bedroom, it's sort out the valuables, the cigarette cases, the leather wallets, empty the purses. In short, swipe the lot!*

The Longuets' dining room, an hour later. The roast still hasn't been served. The guests are, politely, beginning to show their impatience. SÉVERINE *keeps looking anxiously towards the kitchen. Suddenly.*)

GUEST: Can you smell something burning?

(SÉVERINE *gets up and makes for the kitchen. In the kitchen, which is full of smoke, she takes the charred roast out of the oven. Mortified, she looks at the maid's apron and cap left on the tile floor, then at the window, wide open to the dark night.*)

54

SEVENTEEN

*A chilly morning at dawn. The 'Terrot' is racing along the highway.
The 'booty', shoved into bags, carelessly wrapped, is all over the place
– in the back of the side-car, on Janine's lap.*

*They speed through a little town which is still fast asleep. They pass an
abandoned old fishing boat run aground, there's a waste land. At last,
RAOUL stops the bike. There's no one around. He shoves his driving
goggles back on his forehead, which is blue with the cold. JANINE
stays sitting in the side-car, utterly numbed. Like RAOUL, she stares
blankly at what's before her. The beach, endless, and the sea,
completely grey. It's obvious this is the first time either of them has ever
seen it. Silence, then:*

RAOUL: How d'you like it?
JANINE: I didn't think it'd be that colour.
> (*Now, the sun's out, warming everything up.* JANINE, *in a
> black swimsuit, is running along the beach, plunging into the
> breakers, splashing about in the waves.*

> *In a hollow amongst the rolling sand dunes, between the sea and
> the fields, are two tiny orange tents. One of them's for sleeping in,
> the other's a store for the stolen goods. In front of one of the tents,*
> RAOUL, *in his underpants, with a towel around his shoulders, is
> soaping his face with a shaving brush, soap all over his face,
> except for his nose.* JANINE *creeps up on him unawares, and
> jumps on him, all wet against his naked back. He hasn't heard
> her approach, and yells out in shock.*)
RAOUL: Bloody hell! You're a real pain, you are! I've gone and
cut myself now!
> (*They fight playfully, laughing and larking about. He runs after
> her, trying to flick her with his towel.*)
Wait till I get you! Little beast! What a rotten trick!
> (*He finally brings her down and sits astride her.* JANINE *is
> helpless with laughter.* RAOUL *points to his upper lip.*)
Did you notice? I'm growing a moustache!
JANINE: (*Laughing*) Oh don't, moustaches are ugly!

55

RAOUL: It's not ugly at all! In another two weeks, I can turn up in town, and no one will recognize me! I'll be 'incognito'!

JANINE: So?

RAOUL: Then we can get a real motorbike, and have a really great time! (*Puny, with his pale slim body and skinny, hairy legs, he lets out an almighty savage howl.*) Haven't you ever seen a *Tarzan* film?

(*In the neighbouring field, a* FARM WOMAN – *her heavy bulk encased in a brown sweater – is taking the cows to pasture. She spots the pair of them in the dunes – two slight, pale and naked bodies, which, just at that moment, are closely entwined. Her face is full of curiosity and disapproval . . .*

Evening. A camp fire. Three rocks, a pile of twigs, a workman's billy-can. JANINE *is cooking up some grub. Crouched down, she blows on the embers to stir up the fire. She's wearing an old pair of shorts over her swimsuit. She could be Harriett Anderson in* Summer with Monika. RAOUL *appears over the top of the sand dune with a bulging, battered old haversack, which he flourishes proudly.*)

RAOUL: Hey, I found an oyster bed!

(*Then he stops short, as if deeply moved at the sight of her. She's so naturally graceful, full of charm. He comes up to her, then sits*

down a few feet away, just so he can look at her. She smiles at him as she goes on with her task. A fleeting smile, bright and precarious as happiness.

A thousand stars in the sky. In front of the camp fire, RAOUL *gently holds* JANINE *close to him, then looks up into the sky.*)

RAOUL: Doesn't look like there's anyone up there!

JANINE: No? So what's the point of all those stars?

RAOUL: Well, none. That's the point. They don't have to work. They're like us. They shine, they're beautiful, and that's it. They're all like you, gorgeous. While down here on earth, everyone's working their arse off, aren't they?

JANINE: Mmmm . . .

RAOUL: No. That's what's so great! Not having to work, not having to do anything. That's the life!

JANINE: If that's what it's all about, that's what I want. Is that how you're going to make it for us?

(*He puts his arms round her. She snuggles against him. Her heart is beating fast. The profound pleasure of long-drawn-out nights.*

Daytime. The dunes. An oval object, half buried in the sand.)

JANINE: Come and look at this!

(*Her eyes are bright with excitement. She picks the thing up.*

RAOUL *joins her, out of breath. The moustache is coming along:
a little growth of bum fluff which, ironically, makes him look
even younger.*)

RAOUL: Watch out, be careful! It's a grenade! (*He takes it and
examines it closely.*) It's a Yank grenade!

JANINE: Will it still work?

RAOUL: Let's see ...

(*Like Errol Flynn in* Objective Burma *he takes the pin out, and
throws it. They lie flat on the ground. Boom! Explosion. Cattle
bellowing. A stampede. Result: in the next field, the cows are
going crazy. The* FARM WOMAN *rushes towards them as fast as
she can.* RAOUL *and* JANINE *take off.*)

FARM WOMAN: Nudists! You're disgusting! You think I didn't
see you, the other day, don't you? You filthy animals! (*She's
beside herself with hate.*

Morning. The sand dunes. Lying flat in the sea grasses, JANINE
*is watching something: a rabbit, which she traps, taking it quite
unawares as it comes out of its warren. Pleased with herself,*
JANINE *gets up, brandishing her catch by the ears. At that same
moment,* RAOUL *can be seen in the distance, coming along the
road on his bike, no doubt on his way back from a trip into town.
At the familiar sound of the bike,* JANINE *looks round, a
radiant smile on her face ... but not for long. She sees the* FARM
WOMAN *crossing the field towards her, leading a small band of
policemen.* JANINE *lets go of the rabbit, which runs off without
waiting to see what happens next.* RAOUL *has seen everything
from where he is. He shoves his bike behind some bushes.
Helpless, he's witness to it all, sees everything:* JANINE's
*desperate dash towards the beach, with the police close behind,
the violent struggle as they catch her half-way down the slope, the
farm woman's satisfaction, the police pulling down the tents,
trampling all over their belongings, Uncle Rouleau's hand-
drawn portrait.*

*On the road, the bike roars out of its hiding place and disappears
round a corner.* RAOUL *makes his escape.*)

EIGHTEEN

Young girls' faces. Some of them are almost children. Sullen. Obstinate. Tense. Fierce. Drawn features and dark-ringed eyes, from over-indulgence in secret pleasures. Grey aprons. Rubber galoshes. Standing to attention. It's as though they are posing. (Amongst them, JANINE. Much thinner. The sopisticated hair-do is gone: she's in pigtails again. Nuns' faces. Some of them are gentle, patient. Others are hard, intractable. They too assume a pose.

An asphalt yard. A solitary, rather weedy tree. A barrack-like building. A rehabilitation centre for delinquent minors. Around thirty girls, then another ten nuns and the MOTHER SUPERIOR, are grouped together for 'the photograph', around a blackboard on which is chalked: 'Bons Pasteurs de Saint-Avit'.

One of the 'wards', MAURICETTE (sixteen years old), a striking brunette with a headstrong look about her, is taking the photograph. She's looking through a Rolleiflex on a tripod and directs operations with a voice that is hoarse, sensual and imperious.

MAURICETTE: Mother Éliane, I can't see you. More to the left.

(*The nun moves to the right.*)
No, to 'my' left . . . that's it.
(*Then* MAURICETTE *has a go at* JANINE.)
Don't stand there looking like a pumpkin! You're tall, so put
yourself behind the others, at the back!
(JANINE *does as she's told.*)
No, not there. Behind Kebadian!
(JANINE *doesn't know whether she's coming or going.*
MAURICETTE *is impatient.*)
All right. Don't anybody move! Stay just as you are, that's
perfect. (*She conscientiously checks that everyone's in the right
place. The imperious yet appealing expression of a headstrong,
difficult child; the natural authority of a 'leader'.*) Concentrate.
Keep still. Watch for the little birdy.
(*Everyone keeps still. Click.*)
There we are!
(*A few moments later,* MAURICETTE *and* KEBADIAN, *her
pal, are carrying away the benches used for the photo. In the
middle of the yard, the 'Rollei' is still on its tripod. It's a curious
object, like a little black scaffold.* JANINE *is prowling around it.
She takes a quick look through the viewfinder.* KEBADIAN
alerts MAURICETTE *to Janine's movements. Immediately*
MAURICETTE *puts down the bench she's carrying and yells at*
JANINE, *who jumps.*)
You touch that, and you'll feel the back of my hand! (*She
gives a tough, arrogant smile.* MAURICETTE *and* KEBADIAN
snigger. JANINE *beats a retreat, shoulders hunched up. Utter
loneliness.*

*The sick bay. Vaccinations: diphtheria, polio, tetanus. They
make the injections in the boniest part of the shoulder – where it
hurts most.*)

NUN: Keep in single file. Those of you who are more developed
should keep your vests on.
(*The 'wards' comply, shuffling forward in single file. Most of
them are wearing vests.* JANINE *folds her arms across her chest
to cover herself. It's hot and sweaty.* MAURICETTE *takes off
her overall, quite unembarrassed at exhibiting her full, well
developed breasts. The other girls look, impressed. General*

60

admiration. The NUN *who's supervising comes up to her.*)

NUN: What did I just say, Dargelos? Where's your vest?

MAURICETTE: What about it? I need a bit of an airing, you know!

(*Laughter. General hubbub.*)

NUN: I'm warning you, Dargelos. Otherwise there'll be trouble. I'm telling you to put your vest back on.

(*As she says this, she wags her finger in the girl's face.*
MAURICETTE *makes as if to bite it: 'Grrrr.' The* NUN *jumps back. They all start making a humming sound with their mouths closed: Mmmmmmmmmmm . . . Mmmmmmm. The nuns shout at them to be quiet. Intrigued,* JANINE *twists her neck round to see what's going on. She doesn't see the syringe which a dumpy little* NUN *quickly jabs into her.*)

JANINE: Ouch!

NUN: Pipe down, now, girl. It's not going to kill you . . . and that which doesn't kill us makes us stronger.

(JANINE *grits her teeth.*

The refectory. Evening meal. Perched on a little platform,
JANINE *is reading aloud to her companions: Fenelon's*
Adventures of Telemachus. *Conversation is not allowed at the table; all that is allowed is the eating of shepherd's pie. But there's a lot of clandestine activity going on under the table. Barter time. A sallow-looking girl, with a 'merit' badge pinned to her overall, ogles her neighbour's shepherd's pie and offers her an issue of* Songs of the Year. *Quite keen, the other girl offers her half of her portion. The sallow-looking girl gestures greedily with her chin: All of it! The nun on duty claps her hands. Immediately another girl stands up and takes* JANINE's *place at the reading stand. Going back to her place,* JANINE *sees that someone's stolen her dessert. All the other girls have an apple at the side of their plates.* JANINE *looks around her, then under the table. She gives up. She catches the exchange of mocking looks between* KEBADIAN, *who's next to her, and* MAURICETTE, *sitting opposite.*)

KEBADIAN: What's up, Castang? Can't find your dessert?

JANINE: (*Straight*) That's right.

KEBADIAN: Well, don't bother looking any further, ducky.

61

Here you are!
(*With a provocative smile* KEBADIAN *throws the apple she's just eaten to the core on to Janine's plate. The laughter spreads around the room.* MAURICETTE *watches for what'll happen next with lively curiosity.* JANINE *doesn't hesitate. She simply takes her fork and deliberately jabs it into Kebadian's hand. Stupified silence.*)

JANINE: Next time you want something, you can ask for it!
(KEBADIAN, *open-mouthed, looks at her hand, then over at* MAURICETTE.)

KEBADIAN: (*Stammering*) D'you see what this little bitch did to me?
(MAURICETTE *shrugs her shoulders fatalistically, rather amused. Then* JANINE *is knocked off the bench by* KEBADIAN, *who hits her with an empty plate. She rolls on to the floor.* KEBADIAN *jumps on top of her. They slap and punch each other.* JANINE, *violent, gives as good as she gets.* MAURICETTE *follows the fighting with interest. The 'wards' all beat out a rhythm on the table with their fists: 'Kill her! Kill her!' The nuns rush in. They drag* JANINE *and* KEBADIAN *roughly down the stairway to the cellars, which are used as punishment cells.*)

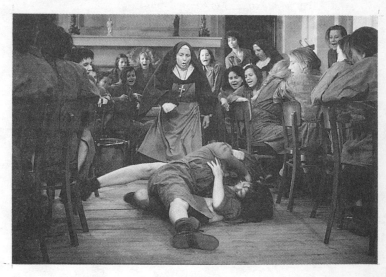

NUN: Eight days each for you two! That'll teach you!
(*Two 'cells', side by side. The wooden doors slam shut.
Immediately* KEBADIAN *starts beating against the walls.
Screaming – no words, just sheer rage.* JANINE *in her cell, her
face bruised; she sits on the hard wooden pallet-bed and stops her
ears with her hands.*

Night. KEBADIAN *has stopped screaming.* JANINE *isn't
sleeping. Lying on the bed, she nibbles at a bit of dry biscuit. She
thinks about* RAOUL, *humming under her breath 'A Little Night
Music'.*)

NINETEEN

Daytime. With a stone JANINE *scratches a mark across the second of
eight vertical lines she's etched into the cell wall – eight lines, for eight
days. The door opens.*

NUN: You're coming out.
(*A few moments later,* JANINE, *accompanied by*
MAURICETTE, *follows the* NUN *through the damp corridors
along the ground floor.* JANINE *has no idea what's going on.*
MAURICETTE *explains to her in a whisper.*)
MAURICETTE: They want a photo for their album. I asked for
you as my assistant. I told them you knew all about taking
photographs.
JANINE: Gosh! You've got a real nerve, haven't you!
MAURICETTE: You need it! When they need you for something,
you can get anything you want.
JANINE: So you got me? (*She smiles, delighted. With her black eye
and bruises, the smile makes her look even odder.*

The dormitory. Night.)
MAURICETTE: That's my trouble – I like having a good time, a
laugh, living it up, too much.
(*Silence, a far-away look.*)
There were times when I was with Raymond he made me
come so much I just couldn't take any more.
JANINE: The most I've ever been in love was when I was nine. It

63

was a Jerry in the Kommandantur. He had such nice hair and a really gentle voice. I think he fancied my mother. He said that I was a very special person.

(*She falls silent, lost in her memories.* MAURICETTE *lets her be.*)

Later on, the men I went with weren't able to do much for me.

MAURICETTE: Have you had a lot of men?

JANINE: (*Blasé*) Quite a few.

(*Silence.*)

MAURICETTE: (*Whispering*) D'you mind if I come into your bed?

JANINE: No.

MAURICETTE: Then I'll come over.

JANINE: OK.

(MAURICETTE *gets in beside her. They huddle together, starved of tenderness.*

The next day; they're working on the 'set' for the photo in a corner of the refectory. JANINE *hands a crucifix to* MAURICETTE, *who's perched on a ladder, next to a grey velvet curtain.*
MAURICETTE *arranges the crucifix, then looks over the effect as a whole.*)

JANINE: Is it true you killed your step-father?

MAURICETTE: Honestly! The way people talk! I beat him up –
there's a difference, you know! He just wouldn't leave me
alone, the bastard, kept trying to touch me up. Morning and
night, as soon as Mum had her back turned. For a year I
didn't dare say anything, I felt paralysed. Then one day,
guess what he did? He actually went and put his hand down
my knickers . . . So I hit him with a hammer – hard! (*She
mimes the action with the crucifix, then she comes down from the
stepladder and goes over to look through the viewfinder of the
'Rollei'.*)

JANINE: The others say it was your boyfriend who gave you the
'Rollei'.

MAURICETTE: Yes, it's true, it was Raymond.

JANINE: And that's what he gave you for sleeping with him?

MAURICETTE: You must be joking! Raymond never had to give
me anything so I'd sleep with him! He's the one who taught
me all about photography. I used to do the cleaning for his
parents. He nicked the 'Rollei' from his dad's shop!

JANINE: A token of his love, then!

MAURICETTE: (*Smiling*) Yes, that's it.

JANINE: What's he like, this Raymond?

MAURICETTE: He's fantastically good-looking! I used to have a
photo. Sister Marie-Odile took it, bloody cow! Oops, here
she comes!
(*The arrival of the* MOTHER SUPERIOR *and Sister Marie-
Odile, excited and all spruced-up, cuts short this exchange of
confidences.*)

MOTHER SUPERIOR: Well, girls? All set up?

(*Semi-darkness. Click of the switch. The enlarger projects
Mauricette's photo: the* MOTHER SUPERIOR *and Sister Marie-
Odile in a very official-looking pose. The photograph is pretty
grim, but* JANINE *is thrilled to bits.*)

JANINE: Pretty good!

(*We are in the 'darkroom', a cupboard under the stairs.*)

MAURICETTE: There's too much contrast.

JANINE: What d'you mean?

MAURICETTE: The dark areas are too black and the light areas are too white. Look, here. The Mother Superior's cap is much too bright; it's like snow.

JANINE: (*Anxious*) We'll have to do something. What are we going to do?

MAURICETTE: (*Shading with it in her hand*) If I do this with my hand, I reduce the amount of light going through, d'you see. That softens the white – it's more subtle like that – and for the dark bits I do the opposite, I bombard it with light.

JANINE: Is that why it's called a shot? Because you bombard it? (MAURICETTE *has never thought of it like this.*)

MAURICETTE: Yes, that's right.

JANINE: (*She is convinced*) It looks a lot better now. (*A pause; then, enthusiastically:*) You're great at explaining things! (*Suddenly, looking at the print:*) Watch out, it's getting too dark!

MAURICETTE: You're right.

(*She busies herself fixing it. Janine's face is attentive. Learning, learning, learning.*

They come out of the cupboard-darkroom. MAURICETTE *mimes framing a photo with her hands.* JANINE *chatters on.* MAURICETTE *gently puts her arm round her shoulders. They pass* KEBADIAN, *who's just been let out of her cell, without seeing her, and she looks after them, with a stony expression.*)

> What did she do then,
> That little swallow?
> She stole from us
> Three bags of corn.

(*The 'fresh-air outing'. The Bons Pasteurs 'wards' pass through the doorway in crocodile, all singing together. Four sisters bring up the rear. The concierge, surrounded by her brood of kids, looks them over, and her little girl throws stones and shouts out.*)

LITTLE GIRL: Lazy-bones! Lazy-bones!

(MAURICETTE *and* JANINE *are inseparable; they're singing heartily.*)

KEBADIAN: (*Bellows out*)

> Go along now, go along,
> The last one, the last one,
> Go along now, go along,
> The last one's out!

66

(*The photos are ready as ordered.* JANINE *taps at the Mother Superior's door. No reply. She enters. On the table, her file: 'Castang, Janine'. A slim folder. Administrative documentations. In a few words, her life is told: Borderline case . . . furtive regard . . .* (JANINE *twitches*) . . . *psycho-moral . . . first periods at fifteen . . . faculty for self-esteem seriously under-developed . . .*

Faculty for self-esteem seriously under-developed? A handwritten letter takes her eye. The Longuets' headed notepaper. Blue ink, pretty handwriting. SÉVERINE!)

SÉVERINE'S VOICE: I never, however, took advantage of my position in any way. At least, I believe that to be the case. On the contrary, I tried to establish a relationship of friendship and trust between us. There were even times when we joked together like real friends. I am both astonished and deeply hurt. Especially hurt.

(*Feeling deeply guilty,* JANINE *stops reading. A phrase in red ink is scrawled at the top of the letter: 'Further offences to be taken into account'.*

The cardboard workshop. JANINE *joins* MAURICETTE, *who is folding the cardboard into boxes. She sits down next to her friend, placing something on the table.*)

JANINE: A present for you!

(*Raymond's photo. A good-looking kid, around twenty-five years old.*)

MAURICETTE: Oh! It's Raymond! That's great of you!

NUN: (*Loudly, to stop the chattering*) Dargelos!

JANINE: (*Taking a cardboard box and, whilst she works, continuing in a whisper*) I've been reading your file. Your step-father wants to withdraw charges. You'll be seeing the magistrate next month.

(*Silence.*)

MAURICETTE: I don't give a damn. I'll have got out of here by then anyway.

JANINE: (*Panicking*) Have you got a plan?

MAURICETTE: I'm working on it! They can all go and get stuffed!

NUN: (*Loudly*) What did I just say, Dargelos? No more

67

chattering!
(*Silence.*)

JANINE: You'll take me with you, won't you? If you really mean
it?

NUN: Castang!

JANINE: (*Loudly, beside herself*) SHHHHIIITT!
(*The two girls look at each other and crease up laughing.*

Municipal sportsground . . .)

TEACHER: One, two, THREE, four. One, two, THREE, four.
(*The 'wards' are doing gym. One of them puts up her hand:* Can
I go to the toilet, Sister? *Permission is granted. She makes for
the changing rooms and opens the door. A scream. In the toilets,*
KEBADIAN *has slashed her wrists.*

The MOTHER SUPERIOR *and the nuns come rushing up from
the edge of the sportsground. Two men in white uniforms are
taking Kebadian's body, wrapped in a sheet, out of the changing
rooms. Two self-important-looking men are conferring
secretively, in low voices next to a van. The faces of the 'wards'
are bewildered.* JANINE *and* MAURICETTE *are overwhelmed.*

What did she do then,
That little swallow?

*Another 'fresh-air outing'. Youthful voices. Little clouds of steam
as they open their mouths. Well wrapped-up. This morning, the
concierge's daughter is in a good mood. She's not throwing stones.
Instead, she gives a friendly wave.*)

LITTLE GIRL: Goodbye, goodbye.
(JANINE *looks at her in passing, tense as a cross-bow.*
MAURICETTE *assumes a false air of calmness. Slung across her
back the 'Rollei', in its beige leather case, swings along to the
rhythm of her walk.*

Crossing the small market town.)

She stole from us
Three big bags of corn.

(*A side street. A parked car. Raymond is at the steering wheel,
sullen, as though he thinks his expression makes him look more of*

68

a man . . .)

Go along now, go along,
The last one, the last one,

(Below, the 'wards', who are crossing the road, in a crocodile . . .)

Go along now, go along,
The last one's out.

(Two hoots of the car horn. The signal. MAURICETTE *looks at* JANINE.)

MAURICETTE: Come on!

(They rush into a side street. Whistles are blown. There are two nuns at their heels, chasing them for fifty yards at full speed. One of the nuns stumbles, falling flat on the ground. The two 'escapees' are picked up by Raymond's car. He makes a spectacular U-turn in front of their dumbfounded mates. The car disappears round the corner, the horn blowing.

Full pelt along the narrow country roads. Out of the car windows sail their overalls; no regrets. RAYMOND *has thought of everything. A change of clothes, which they lose no time wriggling into – for* JANINE, *a soldier's shirt and trousers. A thermos full of coffee and some grub: an enormous ham sandwich, another with roast beef, another with jam. All the things they've almost forgotten eating. They stuff their faces.* RAYMOND, *with a slight smile on his face, is quietly pleased with himself. He drives as though on a racetrack . . .*

RAYMOND: If we keep this speed up, we'll be in Paris by tomorrow night. There's no point going slow. I held up my father's shop.

MAURICETTE: *(Thrilled)* Again?

RAYMOND: Again! And I'll go back as soon as I can and clean him right out!

MAURICETTE: In any case, you could never rip him off as much as he did other people on the black market.

RAYMOND: Yes, but this time round I did pretty well! The boot's full of stuff: two 'Rolleis', lenses, cases of stuff, compacts as well . . . I haven't had time to tot it all up yet!

*(*MAURICETTE *looks at* JANINE. *She wants* RAYMOND *to*

69

make a good impression on her friend. But JANINE *isn't
listening. She's simply miles away . . . The countryside rolls by.
She tries to read her future in it.*

*Late afternoon. A woodland path. The fugitives' car, parked
under the trees. On the back seat,* RAYMOND *and*
MAURICETTE. *They just couldn't wait any longer: they're all
over each other, desperately urgent, like there's no tomorrow. It
must have been like that for quite a while.* JANINE *can't take it
any more. Finally she opens the car door.)*

JANINE: *(Muttering)* Well, I'm going for a walk round.
   (From the back, no response. The sound of rustled clothes.
   JANINE *goes down the path, clenched hands thrust deep in her
   pockets.*

*A little later. Dusk is falling. In the distance, the cries of night
birds. We find* JANINE *hunched up, her arms round her knees,
next to a little pond full of reeds. Suddenly, she creases double,
grabbing her stomach, and throws up.*

*Dawn. A small town. A station forecourt. The car draws to a
stop. Having gone to sleep in the back, with clothes over them as
blankets, the two girls emerge, hair all over the place.)*

MAURICETTE: Why are we stopping?
RAYMOND: I've got to go to the station. I'll get a paper.
MAURICETTE: Don't get bigheaded! We're not that important,
   you know!
   (He gets out. The two girls stay behind alone for a moment.)
JANINE: I think I'm pregnant. *(Some announcement!* JANINE
   looks at her friend, not especially proud of herself.)
MAURICETTE: Whose is it?
JANINE: Raoul's. It must have happened when we were at the
   seaside, at Stella Beach. *(Silence; nostalgia.)* The dates and
   everything match up *(Thin smile)* and I'm right up shit creek.
MAURICETTE: *(Sympathizing)* What rotten luck! What are you
   going to do?
JANINE: Look for Raoul.
MAURICETTE: And if you don't find him?
JANINE: God knows! *(With her thumb, she makes a sharp, ironic
   gesture over her stomach.)* Kkchh! Know what I mean?

70

(MAURICETTE *gets her meaning perfectly.*

The rail car arrives. The three of them on the station platform.
RAYMOND *kisses* JANINE *on each cheek twice, then slips some
money into her shirt pocket – kindly, discreetly.*)
JANINE: Thanks.
RAYMOND: Two hundred francs! It's not that much! Well, then,
it's adios.
(*He moves away, leaving the two girls alone together. They look at
each other for quite a while, not saying anything, face to face, then*
JANINE *shrugs her shoulders. There are no words for situations
like this. It may be they'll never see each other again. Suddenly,*
MAURICETTE *takes the 'Rollei' hanging from her shoulder and
puts it over* JANINE'S. JANINE *takes hold of the beige leather
case as though it were a priceless treasure.*)
MAURICETTE: It's so you'll remember. Don't lose it.
(JANINE *nods. Train whistle sounds. The train's about to leave.*)
JANINE: (*Helpless*) Bye.
MAURICETTE: Bye.
(JANINE *turns away abruptly. She clambers on to the train which
is starting to move away and disappears inside.* MAURICETTE
*makes for a bench on the platform and sits down without saying
anything.* RAYMOND *lets her take her time.*)

TWENTY

*A pale morning. The silence of closed shutters. The streets of the little
town are deserted. A bus arrives in the church square and* JANINE, *like
a tired little soldier, gets off. Old* MOTHER BUSATO *is rolling up the
iron shutters of her tobacco kiosk. Huh! She straightens up after the
effort. The big square, the church, the abortionist:* JANINE *is back
where she started . . .*

A few moments later, at the Rouleaus' house, JANINE *is contemplating
what has become of her old corner 'room': a mess, full of cheese boxes. In
the kitchen,* AUNT LÉA, *wearing a dirty apron, her face etched deep
with all her disappointments, almost unrecognizable, takes several
bottles of wine from a square metal crate. She dumps them carelessly on
the tabletop, deliberately on top of Rouleau's drawings. He merely*

71

shrinks back behind his pantograph. He seems even more worn out than he did when she last saw him. And much older. When she speaks to JANINE, LÉA *has that slow and over-deliberate manner common to drunks.*

LÉA: Can you imagine, we actually got a letter from your mother.
JANINE: (*Turning round, pale with emotion*) Honestly?
    (LÉA *goes to rinse a few dirty glasses in the sink.*)
LÉA: Yep. Can't believe it, can you? Me too, I was flabbergasted. Seems she broke up with her Marcello bloke . . . that she's got herself another one now, his name ends with an o too . . . Gino, Giaccomo, something like that. Seems they're living on an island off the coast of Palermo, somewhere round there.
JANINE: Have you got the letter?
LÉA: I can't remember what I did with it.
JANINE: Oh, really?
LÉA: Well, I'm sorry. How was I supposed to know that you would decide to honour us with a visit? In any case, she wasn't writing about you.
ROULEAU: (*Rebellious all of a sudden*) That's not true! She wanted to know all about you! How you were doing at school, if you'd turned out well, if you'd grown! (*To* LÉA:) Why do you have to say such things?
LÉA: Because I'm awful, because I felt like it!
    (*Silence.*)
JANINE: Could I sleep here tonight?
LÉA: There's no room.
JANINE: I could clear the boxes away. I could sleep on the floor.
LÉA: Are you deaf? I just told you: No. She goes months at a time without sending any news, and then when she's in trouble, it's a different story!
JANINE: One night's not asking much.
ROULEAU: The police were round here yesterday. They were looking for you. So you ran away, did you?
    (JANINE *gives up and goes to sit down at the table, pale, almost about to faint . . .*)
JANINE: Is there nothing to eat?
LÉA: No. That's all over and done with as well. No more cooking for me! Finito! Not for you, not for the other old bugger over

there, the useless old sod. (*She stops suddenly, as though embarrassed by what she's just said.*) There's the left-overs from yesterday, they just need reheating. Then you've go to go. That's the best thing, I'm telling you.
(*Silence.*)
Look at the face on her! If you're not careful, it'll stay like that!

JANINE: Like what?

LÉA: Like someone who'll never amount to anything.

(ROULEAU *looks at his wife, then buries himself in his drawing. That's all that matters now. He's just a little more enervated, a little more defeated.* LÉA *looks fixedly at him, as if it was all his fault.*

The back of Mother Busato's shop. The cat's sleeping on the canary cage. JANINE *readjusts her trousers.* MOTHER BUSATO *finishes washing her hands.*)

MOTHER BUSATO: I can't do anything until tomorrow.

JANINE: Why not?

MOTHER BUSATO: It's always better on an empty stomach, in case of complications. In the meantime, I need a deposit. Two thousand francs.

JANINE: I haven't got two thousand.

MOTHER BUSATO: How much have you got?

(Janine shrugs her shoulders.)
What's that you've got? (*She gestures towards the 'Rollei'.*)

JANINE (*Panicky*) It's mine!

(*Authoritatively* MOTHER BUSATO *takes it off her shoulder.*)

MOTHER BUSATO: Let's have a look at it, then.

JANINE: It's worth a lot more than two thousand!

MOTHER BUSATO: That's what you say!

(*She takes the camera out of its case, which she returns, empty, to* JANINE.)
There you are, I don't want that.
(*She goes to lock up the 'Rollei' in a cupboard.* JANINE *sees a display of goods a fence would be proud of. The cupboard door slams shut.*)
Well, see you tomorrow.
(*Janine makes for the glass-windowed door leading into the shop.*)

No, not that way, that's the shop! (*She points to the door into the square.*) That's the door.

(*Night falls on the church square. Holding the empty 'Rollei' case by its strap,* JANINE *is sitting on an abandoned handcart. From time to time she glances over at the Busato shop. What next? A peasant's heavy cart passes. In the back, a noisy dog howls desperately up at her. Suddenly she notices a police van coming out of a little street, which proceeds to make a peaceful turn round the square. Simply a routine patrol, but instinctively* JANINE *gets up. Not far away is the entrance to a small cinema. Refuge. She goes inside. There's a poster up for 'Musique en Tête', featuring Jacques Helian and his band.*

The programme's already started. A Pathé Newsreel. JANINE *sits down in the dark hall. The voice-over commentary is in progress.*)

COMMENTATOR: The troopship *Athos* is leaving Toulon: destination Indochina . . . soldiers from the sixth regiment of marine gunners are embarking . . .
(*On the screen, young recruits are making their way up the gangway of an enormous ship.* JANINE *is suddenly overcome as she sees one of the enlisted men on screen turn round to smile at the camera. The open expression of an unruly child.* RAOUL. *For a moment, he's looking straight out at* JANINE. *She is in tears.*

She comes out of the cinema, ghastly pale. In the square, old MOTHER BUSATO *is emerging from a little street, calmly returning to her shop. The two women exchange glances as they pass, as if they don't know one another.*

The church square, the same night. The tobacconist's shop sign has been switched off. The square is deserted. MOTHER BUSATO *goes off on her moped.* JANINE *is watching her from the shadows.*

Very loud music. It's the introduction to a children's song, full of hope and energy:

> Daddy, Mummy,
> Your child has only one eye,
> Daddy, Mummy,

Your child has only one tooth.

The tobacconist shop is empty. JANINE *slips softly inside and makes for the door into the back room. In three swift, sure moves she breaks the window in the door to the back room with her elbow, turns the latch from the inside and retrieves the 'Rollei'. A quick look around. It's all right; nobody's heard her.*)

JANINE: (*Muttering*) Time to get out of here . . . (*She leaves quickly.*)

(*A road along the coast. In the back of a bus,* JANINE *is travelling to meet her destiny. Gravely, courageously, come what may. It's a clear morning, bathed in glorious sunshine. Happy days are here again.*)

Words appear on the screen as a kind of epilogue:

A few months later, JANINE *had her first ante-natal examination. Thanks to a mirror, she was able to see the shape of her baby in her belly. As the baby was already moving around quite a lot, the doctor said: 'It'll be a lively little creature!'*

Were you aware of the synopsis François Truffaut and Claude de Givray had written when you were working as Truffaut's assistant?

I'd heard a lot about it, but I'd never read any of it. Over the ten years that I worked with François, I'd heard about *La Petite Voleuse* through Claude de Givray, Suzanne Schiffman and others. I was aware of it as a project, but I didn't have any idea of what it was about. Then, one day, round about the time of *Jean de Florette*, Claude Berri told me that shortly before his death François had given him the two scripts he'd never had time to film: *La Petite Voleuse* and *L'Agence magique*, asking him either to direct them himself or to find other directors to do them. That's how Claude Berri come to ask me to make *La Petite Voleuse*. He gave me these legendary thirty pages to read. Straight away, I knew I wanted to make the film, to develop the synopsis into a script. Why? Because all the interwoven themes touched upon in those thirty pages – and there are several – intrigued me and seemed to link up with the set of themes running through my own work: childhood, the transition from adolescence to adulthood . . . Then there were the period and the milieu, which were similar to my own background when I was Janine's age. And there was another basic reason: I wanted to do another film with Charlotte (Gainsbourg). It was 1985, Charlotte was fifteen. By the time the production was set up and the script ready, she'd be exactly the right age for the part (of Janine).

Apart from your work with Truffaut, there were also your own films dealing with the same themes – La Meilleure Façon de marcher *and* L'Éffrontée. *Is there a sense in which* La Petite Voleuse *can be seen as the last part of a trilogy on adolescence?*

There's no question that with *La Petite Voleuse*, I felt it was quite close to some of my previous films, in particular *La Meilleure Façon de marcher* and *L'Éffrontée*, as they are both films that deal with youth, and youth in relation to petty delinquency. In *La Meilleure Façon de marcher*, Bouchitey's apparent deviance borders on transgression. In *L'Éffrontée* there's the underlying problem of self-delusion and compulsive lying, since she convinces herself, through convincing everyone else, that she's going to leave with the young girl pianist. There's deviance, and a kind of transgression involved. In this case the young girl's a thief; again, an area of transgression, and at a tender age. That's why, no doubt that's why, I said yes to Claude Berri after I'd read the synopsis. I felt completely at home with this kind of story.

Except I'd suggest that L'Éffrontée *has a 'gentler' feeling to it than* La Petite Voleuse, *which is much more feverish, darker, more rebellious* . . .

Yes, you're right. In *L'Éffrontée*, Charlotte Castang's got one main problem, which is psychological – her need to be other than she is. She's not got many additional problems. The young girl thief, Janine Castang, has got a lot more on her plate. She's a real delinquent. She ends up brushing with the law, goes to reform school, and could well go on to more serious criminal activity. When François began this project, there was something quite harsh about it, which connected with *Les Quatre cents coups*.

The big difference with Les Quatre cents coups *is that here sexuality is an important factor in the rebellion and development of the main character.*

Quite. But that was in François's synopsis. There wasn't much dialogue in the synopsis, but I retained all those lines that related to sexuality. When Janine is trying to get out of the mess she's got herself into, she says to the priest, 'Ask me for anything you want. I'll say 'yes', and then you can let me go', or when she says to the forty-year-old guy, the first time they meet, 'If we see each other another five times, the fifth time you're going to ask me. So why don't you ask me right now'. These were aspects of her character that were in François's treatment. There was something else in the treatment which I omitted because I didn't have the time, or perhaps the inspiration, which was a kind of *ménage à trois* with Mauricette and Mauricette's lover. It was a plunge into a quagmire of sexual promiscuity which is quite unusual in François's universe. I didn't go into that. I was intrigued, rather,

77

by Janine's need, which in turn masks a desperate need for affection. When I was young, living in the suburbs, I knew a lot of young girls, around fifteen, sixteen, who had very strong sexual urges. They, like Janine, used to mess around with 'the guys from the glass-works', just like in the film. They were not much more than kids, really – certainly not nymphomaniacs – who were emotionally deprived, whether because of their family life or the milieu generally, and who found 'messing about' – even if they didn't go all the way, they'd get close – a way of compensating for this emotional deprivation.

It's often said that Truffaut is very 'gentle'. Yet what strikes me in his films is the violence of emotions, which can become obsessive. This kind of violence is something one finds again in La Petite Voleuse: *and it intersects with a violence in your own films. I'm thinking here of* Dites-lui que je l'aime *or* Mortelle Randonnée.

You might be right. I can't remember his exact words, but François once said something like, 'The only violence I can accept in cinema is when it's to do with feelings.' And this violence was always there in his films. You only have to look again at *La Peau douce*, *Les Deux Anglaises et le Continent*, *La Sirène du Mississippi*, *La Femme d'à côte*. In these films, the characters really follow their feelings through, wherever that takes them. Once they've become involved, there's no drawing back. François and I had a lot in common, since we were both interested in the same kind of things. There are thematic parallels between *La Femme d'à côté* and *Dites-lui je l'aime*, for example, which are quite striking. I remember well the time I was in pre-production for *Dites-lui que je l'aime*: François, who always kept abreast of my projects, said to me, 'So you're going to do Patricia Highsmith's *This Sweet Sickness*. I'd thought of doing that as a film.' For my part, if I'd come across *La Sirène du Mississippi* or *La Peau douce* before he did, I would have wanted to do them, for sure.

The reform school doesn't figure as strongly in the treatment. You developed that side of it quite a lot.

There were two reasons. First of all, it's a world which I find inspiring. I really wanted to spend a week filming a group of delinquent young girls, girls who were tough and violent. I like that kind of atmosphere. Then there was something very close to my heart: I wanted the end of the film to have a suggestion of hope about it, an excitement, so that Janine leaves with some kind of metaphorical baggage. I chose the camera. As I wanted Mauricette, her friend at the reform school, to be the one who teaches her photography, I had to develop the Bons Pasteurs reform school episode both in length and dramatic impact.

In the film, the adults are none too impressive, are they?

No, not really. But I think that François had no time for heroes, machos, loudmouths. And I feel the same way. I'm just not that keen on characters who only ever do 'positive' things. I like characters with weaknesses, even cowardice and inertia. They just seem more human, more natural, to me. For example, I think that any married man in an adulterous situation would react in the same pathetic way the character in *La Petite Voleuse* does. For me, that doesn't condemn him; rather, it makes him more human.

And that makes Janine's rebellion all the more striking?

Obviously, since adolescents do nothing by halves. It's always interesting to take characters who've already experienced a lot, and have come to accept compromise, and set them against characters who've got no experience as yet, and won't compromise – that is, young people. It's a major theme that I'm always happy to develop.

We really ought to talk a little about Les Quatre cents coups. *You must have thought about it whilst you were shooting?*

I thought about it on two occasions, in terms of the *mise en scène*. One example: I had to do a scene that was similar to a very famous one in *Les Quatre cents coups* – the first experience she has of imprisonment, when she's at the police station. But I never went to see François's film again after I started working on *La Petite Voleuse*. So I had only a hazy, emotional memory of it. But I had François's police station scene in mind when I was doing

79

mine. The second example was something that got cut during the editing. In the film, we don't see her stealing the harmonium; all we see are the consequences, when the harmonium is shown in the secondhand-shop display. But I did shoot the scene where she stole it. And it was rather like when Jean-Pierre Léaud steals the typewriter in *Les Quatre cents coups*, the scene at night where he's staggering under the weight of it. I didn't use it in the end because it was out of sync with the rhythm of the rest of the film.

But what's important to know, as so few people are aware of this, is that François had been wanting to make *La Petite Voleuse* all his life. Originally, *Les Quatre cents coups* was supposed to have a male character, who was Antoine Doinel, and in parallel, or interwoven, a female character, who was Janine. De Givray told me that François had such a lot of material on Doinel that he simply ended up dropping the girl. Which means that all his working life he'd been thinking about making a film about the young girl thief. He'd accumulated a lot of notes and it was supposed to be his next film after *Vivement dimanche!*

You also recognize Truffaut in the scene where the two lads are trying to pick Janine up in the cinema, in the references to Roman d'un tricheur, *the importance of books, etc.*

Yes, there's a little homage to Guitry. The book references were in the treatment; and the character of the middle-aged man who's both the lover and the teacher. Those were François's great themes: love and education.

The film opens and closes with 'childhood' songs. Was that a deliberate choice?

Yes. For the song at the beginning and the end, I was thinking of Vigo and his *Zéro de Conduite* rather than François. Although the film is harsh, violent and rather dark, I wanted it to begin and end with a bit of a swagger, because youth is a time of hope, and when you're seventeen, everything seems possible. I wanted an ending *à la* Renoir, *à la* Vigo, an ending which promises a new beginning, a journey. I wanted the soundtrack to reflect that; something martial, suggesting youth and bravado. So I looked around for marching songs . . . And, quite by chance, I came across 'la meilleure façon de marcher'. I had no intention of being self-referential; it's simply a medley of old marching songs.

And what about the song 'La petite hirondelle' [The little swallow]?

That's something I remembered from school. It's rather cruel, and there's a connection with what's happening in the film, since it's the tale of a young girl who stole three bags of corn.

And is the love of photography she develops a hopeful pointer to cinema, towards an artistic career?

Obviously I thought about François and the well-known relationship between François and Bazin. If he hadn't met Bazin, he would almost certainly have fallen into a life of petty crime – he said so himself. He wouldn't have developed as he did. So I wanted to give a chance to Janine Castang. I didn't choose the cinema, because it seemed a bit facile, a bit obvious. But I could just as well have chosen drawing, painting, music. I don't know. I don't believe Janine will become a great photographer, but at least she takes off with a 'bit of luggage' which means something to her, which she's interested in. It may be that she'll have this camera with her for the rest of her life and maybe she'll become a photographer just as François became a film-maker.

All over the world, there are films which deal with adolescents. La Petite Voleuse *seems to me to be a very accurate portrayal. It's not hamstrung with clichés, it doesn't rely on 'trendy' dialogue . . .*

It was probably the period aspect that saved me. Even if I'd wanted to, I couldn't have used 'contemporary' dialogue since it all takes place in 1950. Rather, I tried to remember how people used to talk when I was young, called on my own memories. In my films – and those who know me always remark on it – people talk the way I do. The language is quite working-class, which is my own background. I relied a great deal on my own memories, and so much the better if that makes it seem authentic.

Isn't there a connection between Janine and the character in

81

Mortelle Randonnée, *who is much older, obviously, but the girl she picks up as a hitch-hiker, Betty, could well be Janine?*

Yes. That's probably why the character of Janine intrigued me so much; as I like characters who break the rules, and the young girl thief is like that right from the beginning. She steals (a little like Marnie, whom I thought about a lot when I was making *Mortelle Randonnée*, the way she's always on the move, changing trains, disguising herself, etc.) and she's always running away, leaving wherever she is at any given time, and usually taking the cashbox with her, like Marnie.

But she doesn't steal the cashbox from the cinema, as she does in the synopsis?

No. I shot it, but didn't use it in the final version of the film. I wanted the cinema, in the film, to be linked to love. It's a meeting place for potential lovers. I think that applies to everyone. A lot of kids have learned to flirt in darkened cinema halls. In the film, it's at the cinema she meets someone who becomes important in her life, and it's at the cinema it all ends, since it's there she sees Raoul, her other lover, leaving for the war. I liked using the cinema as part of the story.

I'd like to talk a little about Charlotte Gainsbourg, who, I think, gives a quite astonishing performance.

She astonished me, even though it wasn't the first time we'd worked together. With *L'Éffrontée* you could see the instinctive gifts she has an actress, but also the grace and freshness of childhood, which obviously helped enormously, given her role. While here, it's clear that she really is an actress. I think she's got a long career in front of her. She's like Katharine Hepburn was at seventeen (I say Katharine Hepburn because she's got the same build, with, at times, the same hint of androgyny, the kind of looks that you can't say are beautiful or not). She's got a side to her that's 'everyday', with an extraordinary facility to move from her own social register into the class of whatever character she's playing (she was actually brought up in the well-to-do 16th arrondissement in Paris). She's totally convincing as a working-class girl. There's another difference: with *L'Éffrontée*, what fascinated Charlotte Gainsbourg was the novelty of the crew, the atmosphere, eight weeks off from school; now she's starting to take real pleasure in her work, in acting, in how to approach a scene, getting it right. I hope we'll soon be seeing her in other films, with other directors. Forman offered her the part of Cécile de Volanges in *Valmont*, but she was already signed up for *La Petite Voleuse*. She has to be seen as an actress, not just a young girl who's made films with her father or with me. She's got innate talent and technical ability, which she's cultivating now, the way any actress does. She's no longer a child prodigy – she's a real actress.

La Petite Voleuse *is also a period film. How did you go about re-creating the fifties?*

My sources of inspiration were very simple: what I remembered were the films of that period – the classics by Duvivier, Autant-Lara, Becker and even the less celebrated films like *Papa, maman, la bonne et moi.* For the region, I thought back to Bresson's *Journal d'un curé de campagne* and all the black-and-white movies of that time. Films featuring François Arnoul; those rather downbeat dramas about abortion: *Des gens sans importance*; Verneuil, etc. That's what I remember from that period. At the beginning, I wanted to make the film in black and white. My memories are black and white. In the end I found a sort of compromise: no bright colours, just greys, beiges and browns. the first colour film I remember seeing came much later, it was Tati's *Mon oncle.* And then I used Doisneau's photographs a lot in creating the atmosphere, the costumes, the sets.

(Interviewed by François Guerif, November 1988)